Bettina

Bettina

THOMAS J. CHILDS

NUAGE
EDITIONS

Cover design by Terry Gallagher/Doowah Design.
Printed and bound in Canada by Marc Veilleux Imprimeur.

We acknowledge the support of The Canada Council for the Arts for our publishing program.

Canadian Cataloguing in Publication Data

Childs, Thomas J., 1964–
        Bettina

ISBN 0-921833-60-1

        I. Title.

PS8555.H525B48 1998   C813' .54   C98-901090-2
PR9199.3.C44B48 1998

Nuage Editions, P.O. Box 206, RPO Corydon
Winnipeg, Manitoba, R3M 3S7

To the memory of
my father

"Sex is the tip of an iceberg.
Nine-tenths of love is hiding."
—Norris Gabriel Azuela

*O*ur first time was at night, between Paris and Lyon, 1968. I beheld him through the heady ricochets of arguments about the student protests. I saw him by his window—rather, felt him—burning brightly, silently reading his *Roman de la Rose*. He consumed the book as a starving man would bread, centred on it, his sustenance. He would devour it likewise on each of the Friday nights that followed. Guillaume de Lorris' twelfth-century masterpiece *Le Roman de la Rose—The Romance of the Rose*.

It has been so many years. When I concentrate, focus hard on the distance between us, it seems he is more like the memory of a vivid dream than the recollection of a physical person with whom I passed nights. In one way, he is vague, a reflection in one of my windows. But still, and this has equal force, I feel an ache when his image enters me. I feel his loneliness, and the weight of his sturdy, purpled heart, its sadness—what *Le Roman* does to a true lover's heart! His devotion to the God of Love above all other deities.

It was his devotion I felt first.

∾

The beginning of the end was long ago. By now we must be nearing the middle.

Spencer is irrigating his eye again with the plastic eye cup. The antibiotics Phoebe prescribed are not working. Phoebe is driving, Heaven help us. Her palms are sweating, she's jerking the clutch, gearing too low. For weeks, she's been disconnected from me, her attentions elsewhere. This is understandable.

She is snacking as she drives, eating as she does only when she's upset. A bag of nacho chips, hot salsa, chocolate, cola in formation around her. Food is a distraction, like the little television she fetched from my luggage hold last week: chewing, swallowing, carries her mind away, like the flickering black and white. Starting on Hallgren's tattoo was a diversion earlier. They've planned an upturned horseshoe—apotropaic, symbolic of the moon goddesses, of *yoni*—on the outside of his right ankle. If only Spencer had been able to continue... Phoebe is a mechanic, not a driver.

She pulls too far onto the shoulder to let a car pass, and my front and back wheels hit the deepest part of a pot hole. The impact jars my brittle suspension, jams the eye cup into Spencer's eye socket. Spencer curses, moans. The most talkative cockatiel protests, "My Lord," from its cage, but our passengers remain calm. Soon, Spencer will insist on taking the wheel again, but we're losing daylight, and Hallgren's tattoo will have to wait.

~

Spencer's injury occurred five days ago as he poured boiling water over a tea bag in a cup. The bag filled with steam on the surface of the rising water, the pressure increased, and the seams gave way. An explosion. Scalding tea-fannings, like tiny shrapnel fragments, flew across Spencer's face, into his right eye.

He flushed the eye with water, but stubbornness kept him from telling Phoebe. So he cleaned the fannings off the splash guard by the burner, bit the inside of his cheeks against the pain in his eye, and made more tea. It was a full day before Phoebe noticed the redness and swelling, and diagnosed the infection. By now, her alarm has deepened. She raises her voice when she speaks about the eye, as she insists he see an ophthalmologist, though her tone is not half as high as it would be if she knew how the infection burned, and how the swelling pressed in. If she knew how the pain deepened when Spencer drove, and when the rays of the sun bounced off of the road. Or, if she knew the sight in the eye was failing… Spencer has given excuse after excuse for not going to a specialist, and Phoebe has shot them down. He cherished his lack of U.S. medical insurance until, shortly after boarding, the passenger, Hallgren, offered to pay the medical bills, and suggested turning back to Salt Lake City. When Spencer continued south, away from Salt Lake City, I knew that more than anything, he wanted to lose his eye.

He cried, "For the love of Christ, I live with a physician!" Maybe only the physical pain in his eye can compete in any way with the pain of knowing he and Phoebe are parting.

And I am aching from the road as I haven't since France. This furious pace through intense heat, this race toward exhaustion. We flee and our flight is aimless.

Back when things were better, Phoebe, my surgeon, would sense my fatigue and order Spencer to pull me off the road into a patch of shade. Early on, Spencer learned that Phoebe would not compromise in my care, and bit his tongue when he thought her overcautious. Phoebe would inform any passenger who objected to a delay that they were free to take their goddamned luggage and walk. Phoebe kept me well for twenty months with her mechanical ministrations, but now, she's preoccupied. The quarrelling with Spencer, worries about ophthamologists and blindness.

The strain has given birth to a grim formality. It keeps Spencer from calling Phoebe "Bea," kills the laughter, the friendly teasing. They don't kiss now— perhaps they don't wish to exhume the memories of the kisses in Mexico. The air is so heavy.

Though it is no one's fault. It's a matter of course, one of the transmutations of Eros. In other words, an instance of Fate's propensity for strings of one-liners, Fate's penchant for awful running gags.

What we need is an old-fashioned miracle.

❦

This morning, just south of the Idaho border, Phoebe faxed the youth hostel in Salt Lake City to offer our services. In a half-hour, we received a request to go to San Francisco. It was a slap in the face. Phoebe could not bring herself to reply.

San Francisco. What a thought! The city where she and Spencer started together, the point from which their unravelling would be most obvious—a place where the eardrum-numbing dearth of magic would finish them in a half-minute. They have avoided the Bay Area since the night with Stan—one might say that, ever since the night with Stan, the tacit *raison d'être* of the Bettina Line has been to avoid San Francisco at all costs.

Fortunately, Hallgren saw the Salt Lake City notice too, and had read about us on a computer billboard somewhere. (We have achieved renown in certain circles these twenty months.) Now, we're a day out of Sedona with three passengers—Hallgren and his two friends. Sedona, as good a destination as any.

These are beautiful people travelling in me. Youthful, open, spirited. At Salt Lake City, a band of devoted friends saw them off—splendid, lifelong friends they've made over a four-day stay. They bring to mind the ones who populated Guillaume's garden in *Le Roman*. Hallgren, the billionaire's son: handsome, blue-grey eyed with long curly hair and no visible beard around his fine mouth. He had flowers in his hair where his lover had placed them, he wore fine leather shoes, a bright, flowered shirt, and Joy on the sleeve. That is, his lover, Joy, with red hair down her back, and smooth, fair skin. She sings—commercials, recording sessions—and her curious eyes seem to dance. Her hair laced with gold ribbon. Carrying her little dog with her—it is an uncertain breed, quiet, no trouble, like the faithful lap dog of a Van Eyck canvas. Hallgren and Joy have been lovers for a half-dozen years, first giving themselves to one another on leave from boarding schools. They hold one another in what seems to me a perfect way—by linking little fingers.

And lovely Erika, whose saintly attributes would be a hand mirror and fashion magazine. Perhaps the most beautiful woman I've ever seen, though I can't say why. There's something boyish about her, she's too plump, butchily dressed, there's an awkwardness in the way she carries herself, in the way she speaks. No one of her features by itself—except maybe her lovely, smooth neck—distinguishes her, but there is something about her that Phoebe, especially, finds fascinating, almost drenching. Something beneath consciousness, some unity of apperception—she resembles a paper doll. Maybe her idleness…her utter idleness, the way she's almost active in her idleness, as she sits blue-jeaned, rubbing cream into the smooth skin of her hands and wrists. She fills me with the scent of tear-out perfume pages, *eau de toilette* inserts, as she leafs through her magazines. For Erika, leafing absently through an Italian *Vogue* is the same as reading scripture.

∾

Dusk. The birds are singing a goodnight song from their cages. We're a few hours from the Arizona border on Highway 89, not far from Panguitch. Spencer has taken the wheel from Phoebe, and Phoebe focuses her attention onto Erika, who believes she needs to change the colour of her hair from its present reddish-blonde to black. After the San Francisco scare this morning, going to Sedona is a reprieve, one in a long line of postponements—how long can we avoid California? How long can we keep this pace? Still, thank God Spencer is driving. He looks awful. He squints against the pain of seeing out of his eye, and against a headache verging on migraine. His nails are too long, his hair trails in his face. Shiny skin, the dull thrumming of intestinal gas. It's as though he's collapsing—I sense a deterioration even since Salt Lake City.

Near the back, on their sleeping mat, Hallgren lies with his head in Joy's lap. From the driver's seat, Spencer only just hears Joy's soft singing. It drifts in and out of him, and the sound of love increases his pain. Nearer to him, nearer to my front, Phoebe and Erika sit side by side in easy chairs. Spencer hears Erika say, "I would never work at a job as long as I had enough clothes…" She runs her hand across Phoebe's sleeve, because she is an unabashed toucher, because she seems to communicate, more than in any other mode, through bodily contact. "What kind of silk is this?" she says. Another of Phoebe's heart-to-hearts, Spencer thinks, and feels a sensation like nausea. He recalls other times Phoebe has sat in the same chair and conversed with passengers through the dusk, into the night. In his pain-altered state, he has the intuition of having misplaced something, and then he needs to speak. For all kinds of reasons, he needs to speak. He knows that if he doesn't speak, he will scream. He says, "Phoebe, how far do you want to go?"

And she says, as if ready and waiting with her response, "I don't know, we'll see how we feel." Her eyes don't leave Erika. "How far do you want to go?" No doubt these puns are unintended. Though, still, Spencer hears the smile on Phoebe's lips, and suddenly entertains the idea of driving all night. He knows that if we stop, he won't sleep.

"We'll see how we feel," he says.

A half-hour passes, and we lose the last of the light outside. The birds are asleep. Hallgren and Joy pull the curtain closed around themselves, and begin quietly making love. Phoebe and Erika lean very slightly closer.

Spencer struggles to keep me on the road, and fails to notice that we are following the same Airstream motor home we followed yesterday in Idaho, and two days ago in Oregon. I feel an ominousness in the coincidence, a discord. In daylight the most striking thing about this thirty-three foot silver cylinder is its windows, the way they are silvered on the insides. When you try to look inside, you only see yourself. Yesterday and the day before the Airstream eclipsed our view of the road ahead off and on for hours, as it drank its way relentlessly forward from two enormous gasoline tanks. We stopped first for refuelling both days, so I could never glimpse its inhabitants. But Spencer doesn't notice. He's too intent on hearing the conversation behind him.

In which Erika bitches entertainingly about her lack of a love life, about the seemingly endless sexual drought that has settled down upon her. "Is one lover so much to ask for?" she says. It occurs to Spencer that this woman, Erika, has stated no sexual preference, and finally, he identifies the gnawing in his gut as a subclass of his more general fear of losing Phoebe. His hands feel very tight on my wheel.

Phoebe tells Erika that the trick is not getting stuck on one person, that obsessing is where the trouble always starts. "Sexual love is a fraud," she says. "A carnival ruse. The idea of love and sex mixing: girl, it's nothing but a telemarketing scam…"

Erika wants to how many times Phoebe and Spencer dated before they had sex. "If you mean capital-S Sex?" Phoebe says. "It was our second date. Though we haven't done it since…"

"Really," Erika says.

And Spencer murmurs, "We're sexual in our own way," and laughs out loud. The laughter is a relief. "Nothing," he says when Phoebe asks him what's so funny.

Erika wants to hear the story of how Spencer and Phoebe met, and this pleases me, because the story completes itself a bit more each time I hear it. I've heard Spencer tell it, and Phoebe, I've heard them tell it as a duet. The first full telling I heard was on a cool night last autumn in West Virginia, after many hours of driving had turned Spencer toward reflection, and a passenger—a former business executive who insisted he was heading for the sea to find a mermaid—asked to hear. The second time, it was Phoebe, in Alabama, under the awning off the side of me, over a plate of lentil stew. Taking fragments into account, I've probably heard the story of their meeting a dozen times. Each time is neither different nor the same as any earlier telling. The inflections change according to circumstance. A new word there, a detail dropped or added. The story grows and transforms itself as elements are born and others die. Though still, I feel the story must be riddled with holes. Surely their troubles today should be discernible in that first meeting, surely something was wrong from the start.

Yes, this telling is different from all the others. As Phoebe begins, there's an edge to her voice—an irony or mourning, or a fatigue bordering on bitterness.

"Two years ago," she tells Erika. "At the Castro Theatre in San Francisco. The Wurlitzer guy rose out of the stage, and began his performance. Spencer was from Red Deer, Alberta then—Canada—he worked with a funeral director. He'd tagged along to San Francisco with his lover, Jennifer. She sold textbooks. I was in from Montreal for a surgical convention..."

"You're a doctor?" Erika says.

Phoebe nods.

"Why would you want to be a doctor?"

Phoebe smiles, but doesn't get into it. "I was living with a man named Anthony then, and he had come with me. He was tired of going to dinners where he had to talk to the others surgeons' wives. I was at the end of four days of lectures. I had attended everything I could find about laproscopic surgery. He talked me into seeing a movie at the Castro, and the Wurlitzer guy..."

"You mean a Wurlitzer organ?" Erika says.

Phoebe nods. "About ten minutes before the movie starts, you hear the beginning of 'The White Cliffs of Dover,' and then a guy in a suit, attached to a Wurlitzer, rises up out of the stage. At first he doesn't play too loud, though he grabs great handfuls of keys, and moves around his foot pedals like he's figure skating. Anthony actually looked up from his book. Anthony always read poetry to himself before a movie started—he wasn't much of a date.

"Anyway, the Wurlitzer guy starts up, but I can still hear the man behind us trying to talk his sister into moving west from Maryland. He sounded like he wanted her in San Francisco very, very badly. And this fifty-something guy beside me who I decided had probably had his teeth capped in about 1970 and come to California from North Dakota. Twenty-five years later, there in the Castro Theatre, he was telling his friend about his day of driving the shuttle bus from SFIA. The Wurlitzer guy moved into another song—the cinema crowd didn't seem to be paying much attention. I looked at the couples, gay and straight, the singles, the groups of three or four. Stragglers took the last seats, set their popcorn carefully on the floor as they settled themselves. Anthony was people-watching too, but all of a sudden it occurred to me that he looked mean."

"Mean?"

"Like he had this sneer on his face. Like he was laughing at people. All of a sudden I felt lonely. And just then, I noticed the organ music was louder. Loud enough now to block out the voices around me. The music seemed very beautiful.

"That's when Spencer and I made eye contact. He was on the other side of the theatre. He had been looking at me, and when our eyes locked the way they did, I felt my heart start to palpitate. I felt my face heat up fifteen degrees, and—it was the strangest thing—I just stopped breathing! He must have felt it too, because his eyes started to dart back and forth between me and the Wurlitzer guy. I guess we were both in shock. The most intimate eye contact I've ever experienced."

Erika says, "Love at first sight?"

At hearing Erika's words, Phoebe feigns retching, but this is a cover. And in the moment of silence I imagine her and Spencer in the cinema, everything around them dissolved from awareness, only one another's eyes… And I think of my scholar again, how he might have quoted Guillaume's *Roman* now, mentioned that the God of Love always poisons his arrows with Beauty, Simplicity and Courtesy, aims for lovers' eyes. My scholar would emphasize the accuracy of the god's aim, the sharpness of the arrow points entering the eyes, leaving no visible wound, lodging in the heart.

Phoebe speaks again, and there's a hint of panic in her voice, like an animal slowly realizing it is caught in a trap. "Spencer's lover offered him the popcorn box, and as he took it from her, he had to look away from me for a moment. That's when I managed to breathe, and then someone nudged me, said something I couldn't hear. It took me a moment to remember I was with Anthony. Looking back at him was awful. This dull feeling, like a strangler's hands taking hold of my neck. And suddenly I knew I was *getting by* in life, nothing more. I was wasting so much precious time. All I could see was Anthony's sneer, and the only thing I wanted in the world was to punch him in the mouth."

Erika giggles.

"The Wurlitzer music had grown so loud, it filled the house. The chords pressed the air in, made it hard to breathe. The organist's hands, everywhere on the keyboard. His tap-dancing feet.

"I felt the man on the far side of the theatre looking at me again. I wanted to look back so badly. My heart was going crazy; I thought I was going into arrest. I had crazy images from my internship: paramedics wheeling heart-attacks into Emerg, and the resuscitation team going to work." She looks at Erika, and her eyes are crazy. "I just can't say the things I was feeling. A kind of longing, it was so strong. And then, somehow, I was looking back at him, and feeling everything open up. I noticed I was smiling. He was blushing. He was red as a tomato.

"The Wurlitzer guy teetered at the top of a final, monumental crescendo as the platform he was on descended back into the stage. He played his last chords, took a bow to acknowledge the ovation, and stepped onto ground level just as the house lights dropped for the movie. I saw Spencer reassuring his lover: 'Nothing's wrong,' I saw him tell her."

Phoebe gives an uneven sigh. "They started running the forecasts."

"Trailers," Spencer says.

Phoebe sighs, and tells Erika, in a confidential way, that there's something wrong with her brain, the way she confuses words. She's always done it, especially when she's tired.

"Some neurons are crossed or something," she says. "Anyway, the trailer was a short with William Burroughs thanking America for its many gifts. Unemployment, social unrest, that kind of thing. Anthony was enjoying it like crazy, and for all I know, it was a terrific short, but I was in the midst of being overwhelmed by the fact that all men were such assholes. I only mention that because I only ever think that all men are assholes when I'm at the very end of a relationship, and it hadn't occurred to me before then that I was at the end of my time with Anthony. It figured there was a fifty-fifty chance the guy across the cinema was an axe-murderer, but I knew I needed to look at him again.

"So, I did, when my eyes adjusted to the dark, and just as I focused on him, he turned and faced me too. This time it was different—more serious, ten times more dangerous. I remember giving a sort of nod, with my eyes as much as my head. He nodded back in the same way, very dignified, respectful. And with that, and as William Burroughs thanked America for neo-Nazism, we took leave of our respective lovers.

"I saw Spencer pick up his jacket and stand up in that crouching way you do in a theatre. I saw him say something to his lover, and I saw the baffled look on her face as she watched him go. So I told Anthony I was tired, and that I'd see him back at the hotel later. He didn't seem baffled at all. He seemed mostly irritated that we'd be taking two cabs back downtown. Anthony was very cheap when it came to spending my money.

"And then I felt my legs wobble as I walked up the aisle, and then I was standing in the lobby facing this guy. I imagined more Emergency Room scenes, and decided I must be dying.

"He said his name, but he stuttered. 'Spencer,' he said. 'Spencer P-Peach.' Hearing his name confused me. I said, 'Spencer Ph-Phoebe,' and I only realized my mistake when I saw the look on his face. I said, 'I mean, Phoebe Spencer.'"

Phoebe leaves her easy chair to put the kettle on for tea.

"Tongue-tied lovers," Erika says.

"Absolutely," Phoebe says. "Verbally cataleptic. We didn't try to speak again as we walked out onto the street."

(I know from Guillaume, through my scholar, that only a con artist escapes the unaccountable anxieties of a great love. The night Spencer told the mermaid-seeking businessman the story of meeting Phoebe, he marvelled at the way he'd never once in his life stuttered before that night. He'd had a nimble tongue, he said, spent his adolescence peeling a thousand grapes without his hands— an adolescence in training for love. With such dexterity, he said, he should never have lost control. But only false lovers chatter freely when love hits them. Love is unaccountable.)

"I couldn't focus," Phoebe says. "I knew what I was doing was crazy, that I should apologize for dragging this guy away from his movie, head back to my hotel, find a group of doctors to get drunk with.

"Spencer hailed a cab driving on the opposite side of the street, and the driver pulled an astonishing, dashing U-turn in the middle of Castro to fetch us. We got in. Spencer said the words, "North Beach?" and I shrugged.

"The driver used a precise staccato. 'Yes! Fine! North! Beach! Just! Fine!' he said, and sailed out into traffic. It was good we had this driver. He was worth watching—Spencer and I could keep our eyes averted from one another. The way he zigged and zagged through traffic was mad. So fast, unafraid. A tall, black man about thirty, with perfect posture, and the most immaculately-pressed white shirt. The dark, thin tie, horn-rims, and shaved head made him look like Malcolm X. The windshield was clean, but in the midst of an elaborate traffic negotiation, he took a tissue from the box on the seat, and polished the glass above and to the right of his view, then ducked into a back lane, rolled down his window, and tossed the wadded Kleenex into a dumpster without slowing down.

"'This is insane,' Spencer said, when we were standing on the sidewalk in North Beach. So I asked him just how insane he actually was, if he saw a psychiatrist, for example. He thought I was joking…"

"You weren't joking?" Erika says.

"Of course not. See, I attract freaks. Every kook who steps onto a transit bus has to sit beside me. Lunatic masturbators in supermarkets, you name it. Apparently I represent sanctuary for the crazy, so naturally, I thought Spencer…"

Indeed, at this moment, Spencer *is* feeling very disturbed. The searing pain in his eye, the sound of Phoebe pouring water from the kettle—he's been uncomfortable with boiling water since the tea bag incident. Though more than anything, he fears he will begin to scream uncontrollably. He considers pulling me over to the shoulder.

Phoebe asks Erika if Hallgren and Joy will want tea. Erika says no, that they'll be gone for a while yet. They like to be alone about this time of day.

What about Anthony, Erika wants to know, was he crazy?

"Not exactly," Phoebe says, "but he was a poet, so almost. Early on, I thought he was a young Leonard Cohen, the way he talked about love and travel. I found it romantic the way he paid such close attention to his dreams when he woke up in the morning. I can see now that he was a windbag. Pretty dull, mostly incomprehensible. As for the dreams thing, I think he was just someone who slept too much. Though it still hurt to leave him in the cinema. It was a terrible way to break up. If I could do it again…"

"I know," Erika says, and seems to means it.

Phoebe sets Spencer's tea beside the steering wheel, and puts one hand on each of his shoulders. "But here was Spencer," she says, as though Spencer can't hear. "These stunning shoulders. And his captivating eyes…" A shudder goes through her as she realizes what she's said. Her hands leave Spencer's shoulders too abruptly, and she steps back toward Erika. She bums one of Erika's cigarettes.

Phoebe begins to dye Erika's hair. She works the dye through the strands, and the smell unsettles Spencer's stomach again. He opens my little window a bit wider.

"We drank beer in North Beach," Phoebe says and applies more dye from the squeeze-bottle. "A number of things became clear for me. A major disappointment, for one thing. My career. I was a surgical resident who'd finished paying off her student loans, I was rising quickly in my field, but, talking to Spencer, I realized the only reason I'd gone to San Francisco was that I'd hoped to feel some echo of the sixties. Just an afterglow, a flashback. But in Haight-Ashbury, I found the parade had passed through so long before that the confetti in the gutters was dusty and pissed-on. I'd arrived very late to a party and everyone had already passed out. Catching up wasn't an attractive option. So I was disoriented. Aimless."

"What were you looking for?" Erika says.

"Something eternal," Phoebe answers, and spreads some Ponds cream on Erika's ear against the dye running. "After I told Spencer about that, he told me he'd come to an understanding of his own. Namely, that he loved to travel, but couldn't bear leisure. The past day he'd been realizing how badly he slept in fine hotels, and how he missed his own cooking when he ate in some of the world's best restaurants. It made him gloomy to wake up and not have to get ready for work. He had taken to calling the places he and Jennifer ate at 'stress-taurants.'"

Phoebe watches the reflections of highway lights on the surface of her tea. "After midnight," she says, "we climbed Telegraph Hill, and looked at the city. Spencer asked if he could kiss me. I thought about it, and said yes. How sweet that tasted! That kiss drove out all the disappointment..." Phoebe needs to stop talking. Erika puts an arm around her. Dye gets on Phoebe's shirt.

I imagine Phoebe and Spencer actually *glowing* on Telegraph Hill—"He who is nearest the fire burn brightest"; that's the way Guillaume put it 750 years ago. They, and my scholar, know the disquieting feeling of giving their hearts to another without division. Irrevocably. Accepting the blessing of the God of Love, allowing him to lock their hearts with small gold keys. To what higher deity can two people surrender than the God of Love?

And they did surrender. So what is it that prevents their delight now? I'm convinced their pain wants understanding, whether it be some catastrophic pain resonating down deep, or a concatenation of lesser ones.

Later, Phoebe says, they wandered too close to the hotel she was staying in. "Anthony was out front, lighting one Lucky Strip off of another…"

Spencer says, "Phoebe, Lucky Stripe."

She says, "We tried to duck out of the way, but Anthony saw us, and there was a chase, though we lost him. So I waited a while, and called him at the hotel."

"What did you say?" Erika wants to know.

Phoebe shrugs. "That I was sorry for wrecking his last night in San Francisco. That I'd fallen in love. That he could have the apartment, and I'd pick up my stuff."

"Enough for one call."

"Spencer called Jennifer too. Then we went for bagels."

Finally, Spencer speaks. He calls back to Erika and Phoebe. "She ordered toasted poppy seed, and half an antelope." Then he fiddles with the stereo—a signal that he's left the conversation again.

"I meant half a cantaloupe," she says. "Time to wash out the dye," she says.

The dye stains the wash-basin black. "We were in the bagel place when we decided to start this bus line," Phoebe says. "We would buy a bus, and it would be our home on-the-move. We'd travel forever, but Spencer would have a purpose. We'd go where we wanted, take a few passengers to help with costs. Our passengers would be our family. Spencer would drive, I'd be the mechanic. We'd be together."

"You were a surgeon and a mechanic?" Erika says.

"No, but I figured people and buses couldn't be all that different. Heart...engine block. Nervous system...wiring. Anyway, driving gives me ulcers."

As Phoebe drapes a towel over Erika's head, it occurs to me that when she drives, it gives everyone ulcers. Erika stands straight. Thirty minutes: the patient's hair changed from red to blue-black. Phoebe pulls off her gloves, and snaps them into the garbage—gesture from her last career. Dye spattered on her shoulder. She takes another of Erika's cigarettes.

"We talked for eleven hours!" she exclaims. "I don't know how many times we said the "L"-word. The world was wide open. We both wanted to make love...though we didn't."

Erika nods.

Phoebe shrugs. "Maybe we already knew."

"Knew what?"

"That part wouldn't work."

Erika doesn't understand.

Phoebe says, "It was dawn. We were sitting about as close together as it was possible to sit in a café booth. If it had been the sixties, we'd have made love five times by now. But Spencer said, 'You know what I'd like? I'd like it if we never had to move from this position ever.' The best thing anyone ever said."

"You just didn't want to make love."

"We'd been making love all night," Phoebe says. "Anyway, sex is the tip of an iceberg. The point is that all the disappointment had gone away, and everything was perfect." I feel Phoebe's pain like I feel the road under my wheels. She is imagining life without Spencer.

Erika holds her.

The curtain around Hallgren and Joy opens. Joy's little dog is out first, nails tapping across the linoleum, eyes curious. Joy goes into the washroom. Hallgren asks if he can put the kettle on.

Phoebe says, "I had to be in Montreal that night. I was on call. Anthony was already gone when I stopped in at the hotel to get my bags. That was good. He'd just have glared at me, not said a word, then turned melodramatically and stared out through the mini-venutians at the city."

"Venetians," Spencer murmurs.

"Spencer came with me to the airport," she says. "And that was that. It was really hard to leave him..." She palms the air upward. "But that's the thing, isn't it? All you have to do is look really closely at the beginning of something, to see the end of it. Everything good is like that."

⌖

I call him my scholar, though I know that he was never mine. A graduate student of mediaeval literature, who left Paris on Friday nights for Lyon to see his parents. Sometimes he travelled with other students, though he felt most alone among close acquaintances. I spent our Friday nights on the road between Paris and Lyon memorizing him: his deep, brown eyes, his blond hair— long, in the manner, the girl told him the last time, of a mediaeval knight. I memorized his nose, which he described as flattened *(s'écrasé)*, though I thought it very beautiful. I memorized the pace of his breathing as he slept, his dreams. The colourful shirts fashionable at the time—though I knew his concern for clothing was glancing. His gaze went inward.

He was happiest reading *Le Roman de la Rose,* and planned his thesis around it. When he read it, he seemed to glow, filling my body with a rare, pure light, causing me almost human pain. He who is nearest the flame... No mortal could have known Love better—and I experienced a state of *joie* with him, the state of perfect sharing with a lover, experienced by the courtly lovers. Perfect knowing. Joy: spiritual, round. Bold.

Until our last night, late in the spring of 1969. I drove him through a rainstorm and he told Guillaume's allegory to the young woman sitting in the seat beside him. A lovely girl, only seventeen or eighteen, almost a child. They had talked about many things, until he began to narrate Guillaume's dream of entering a splendid garden in which the God of Love was holding court. Wandering until he discovered a perfect rosebud, and falling in love with it. How he would have picked it were it not for the opposition of others in the garden.

My scholar told his favourite story passionately, near-bursting, and his story was a form of love-making, transporting the girl out of her world into Guillaume's dream one, onto the inner landscape of pure, spiritual Love. The exalted struggle: one gentle person giving their heart to the other. The graceful love that Guillaume knew. How different courtly love than the catastrophe of courting-as-combat, from the heresy of calling vulgar conquest, of naming some barbaric struggle between predator and sexual prey, "Love."

After midnight. We neared Lyon, and it was plain to me that there would not be time to finish the story before we reached the terminal. So, slowly, with complete attention to safety, I closed my brake shoes against my drums and held them there, so my driver pulled me to the side of the road, and was forced out into the rain to find a telephone to order another bus to come out from Lyon for his passengers.

Though my stunt aroused no end of cursing from the other passengers, my scholar was able to finish his recitation of the *Roman* to the young woman. Even to the tragic conclusion wherein Guillaume de Lorris' dreamer discovers that the rose—purest heart of Love— is unattainable in this world; is, simply, undeniably, impossible. So the young woman was moved. (Such is the power of the *Roman* to change us forever.) When the replacement bus arrived forty-five minutes later, my scholar and the young woman alighted me together, their little fingers linked.

Of course, locking the brakes was my undoing. The unexpectedness of it, added to my age, made me "no longer reliable," so by the following Friday I had been reassigned to an inconsequential run between Paris and Amiens, and my scholar taken from me. Late the next Friday evening, when I should have been warming up in Paris, in exquisite anticipation of my scholar's arrival and boarding, I was dropping shoppers in Oise, leaving grey commuters, like packages, in Clermont.

I moved sluggishly, imagined him stepping onto the factory-new bus. How did he feel when he noticed the brazen upholstery in the sixth row, or when he caught the factory scent after my wealth of mustiness? Did he miss me? And, could a bus fresh off an assembly line possibly appreciate him? Could it care a nut for his fine features or splendid thoughts, even begin to sense his depth of feeling? Or would it toe that factory-efficient line that brooked no emotion, that fascist no-nonsense Newness? Step along now, take your seats, we'll be at our destination on time come Hell or high water... How I detest the spanking New!

The hours that Friday night constituted my object lesson in the impossibility of Love, and the lowest point of my existence. The last of my power seemed to leave me, it was as though everything about me seized. The administration's pessimistic prophesy about my unreliability fulfilled itself. The question I used to ask, "Can the French really die of love, die for love?" was answered that night. Yes! Yes, I believed I really could.

And though he was years ago, my scholar's power resists fading. Even now, though my vocabulary for love is out of date, I feel the world through his words, and through Guillaume's words, which he uttered so beautifully. The kilometres that have raced beneath me! Here on a faraway continent, an ocean between us, I still feel his warmth. Back in France, it's late at night. Is he lying in bed beside his young woman—not as young now, but as fetching—rereading *Le Roman*? Or has he set the book on the night-table, shut out the light, laid his lovely head on the pillow? Is he drifting toward sleep, deepening, recalling strains of our Paris-Lyon rides...?

∾

When Phoebe and Spencer parted at San Francisco International Airport, they did not know when they'd see one another again. The idea of spending days apart now was cruel; they could not bring themselves to consider weeks. The parting kiss at the gate began a flurry of letters, and long, windy cross-country calls. The constant question: when, where, how to reunite.

Spencer says his time without Phoebe was like living in the grip of a fever. Hot, then cold; flushed and perspiring, then pallid and dry. He recalls sitting motionless for long periods, not even moving his eyes, entertaining nothing so discrete as a thought, only feeling waves of a deep, salty desire, then waking with a start to his situation, and falling back to the sighs and shivering.

My scholar would have called this distress a virtue. Real love may come in a flash, he would have said, but elevation to any high station within Love's Court requires the pain of waiting. The point is one of ripening: that which would be bitter and sour, if tasted too soon, transforms itself into something sweet through the torment of separation, and thoughts of the beloved. Love, like any fruit, must ripen.

Indeed, Phoebe and Spencer both say they were deepened by their pain, that it imparted to them a certain gravity, even a kind of nobility. They began to greet others before they were greeted themselves, they dressed with extra care—bought new clothing, polished their shoes, wore flowers the other had sent them, listened to music more closely and for longer periods, felt music more profoundly. Phoebe dusted off her flute after years away from it. They read novels, played with children. Of course Love will cause these things—Love fills its lovers with colour and new perception.

Spencer spent his evenings that summer exhausting himself on a basketball court with his friend, William, a graduate student in theology and philosophy. Afterward, he would sit, winded and strained, and flog himself for things he'd failed to say to Phoebe in San Francisco, and, occasionally, for postponing their love-making.

"Why do you think you didn't make love?" William would ask, and squeeze water over his head from the bottle.

"Isn't it obvious?" Spencer said.

William is patient. "No, not obvious."

"We were afraid we'd crash like a 747. Of course."

"Still not obvious."

"Something might have broken between us."

"Something fragile."

"Yes!"

"*Pothos*." William said. "One of the faces of *Eros*. Unlike *himeros* and *anteros*—*himeros,* the heat of the moment, and *anteros,* relational love, what your lover answers your love with. *Pothos* is the blue rose of romance that pines for the unattainable and impossible. It is the imagination of ideal love, the love no one ever grasps. *Pothos* is spiritual love. It drives you forward; it's the reason you're alive at all."

And Spencer, "Okay then, *pothos*, that's the one." He'd regained his breath by now. "Tell me more about *pothos*, Brother William." Spencer called William "Brother" because William was going to become an Anglican priest.

"Some people risk everything for *himeros*," William said, "or *himeros* and *anteros*. Others deny these two for the sake of *pothos*—they insist on transcendence."

Spencer says that he and William speculated widely on the basketball court near the funeral home. He says speculating was good for him at the time.

∽

Hallgren and Joy have listened quietly while Phoebe tells Erika the story, Joy's little dog a warm ball of comfort in Phoebe's lap. The dog leaves Phoebe's lap and returns to its mistress. Joy wants to know why Phoebe left surgery.

Phoebe shrugs. "My patients' bodies had become so many pancreases and colons," she says. "That was a bad sign. I didn't like how intimate I was getting with my instruments of torture…"

Hallgren says, "Then you were right to leave for a while."

For a while catches Phoebe. She looks Hallgren in the eye, murmurs, "And the Chief of Surgery was an asshole."

"What did *you* leave behind, Spencer?" Erika says.

At first Spencer pretends he hasn't heard the question. It feels to him as though everyone is clustered in very close to him. The group presses in; he wishes it would recede. And he wishes this pain would recede too. It engulfs him entirely, it washes through his whole body. "I played a lot of basketball," he says.

"And you were going to be a funeral director," Phoebe prompts. Her voice sounds constricted. So, talking is difficult for her too.

Spencer knows the only way out of the conversation is to stop for the night, swallow a handful of painkillers, go off by himself. But he does not want to stop driving. So he says, "I prepared bodies for burial, sold caskets and urns. You know…" He hopes they'll let it go.

But Joy is interested. "I don't know if I could do that. I think that would be hard." Spencer says, "It is. It's hard work. You're on call twenty-four hours. I liked it, though. Even if I was too introverted to be a salesman."

"You found Bettina on a sales call," Phoebe says.

"Mmmm."

The others are relentless. They want to know about the sales call during which Spencer found me.

"I was at a woman's house, arranging her husband's funeral. She was Russian, her husband had been Greek. They spoke Bulgarian to one another even after they moved to Canada and learned a bit of English. She was a lovely woman. She had this hairdo, enormous, like a roller coaster. I don't know how she kept it that way." He forces himself off the tangent. He says, "We were sitting at her kitchen table, looking at photos of cremation urns, and I looked out the window and saw the bus."

Me!

"Bettina," Joy says.

"The Greek husband had brought her over from Europe. He and his wife were planning to explore North America and he was fixing the bus up. He was nearly done. She needed paint and tires, not much more. The widow chose a very nice brass urn, and, as gently as I could, I asked if she'd thought of selling the bus. She said "Yes" right away, so I called Phoebe in Montreal from her phone."

"You quit your jobs," Joy says.

Phoebe nods, and there's the trace of a wince. "I wound everything up, and got to Spencer's in four days."

∾

It's after two. We've dropped anchor—they call it "dropping anchor" when we stop for the night because of my size. We're a quarter mile from the main road, a stone's throw from the bank of Lake Powell. It feels good to rest at last.

Though I saw it again just before we stopped. It came and went from our view, like a virago or a recurring dream: the Airstream, like a roll of aluminum foil from a planet of giants. Again, no one seemed to notice. All Spencer could think about—his knuckles were white from gripping the wheel—were painkillers. No one else was looking out at the road. I don't know why the Airstream frightens me so.

When Spencer parked me, he stood and gave a sigh—or less a sigh than a desperate effort to expel his sickness—thought, with mixed emotions, of getting into bed beside Phoebe again. Then he felt Erika stroking his shoulders.

"Boy, they really are fine," she said, and whistled. "Broad, firm…"

I felt Phoebe harden, and then relax as Erika winked, so the lightness of the flirtation came clear. This is Erika: someone who will always take another person by the elbow as she walks with them, someone whose embraces would win all awards, were such things prized.

And now, with my motor stopped only twenty minutes, everything is very quiet. Humans bedded down for the night, the birds silent. Spencer, stuffed full of Tylenol 3s again.

∾

In perfect darkness, my headlights out, nothing distracts me from my reflections. I think about my days and nights as a bright young motorcoach, delivered, in 1938, by the skilled hands of craftsmen at the Renault factory, Billancourt, and launched onto my Paris-Lyon route. The breakdown I faked that night for the sake of my scholar, and the real breakdowns I suffered in profusion afterward. Then, the route I traced over the slow Adriatic

Coast from Rijeka to Baska, after the Yugoslavs bought me.

I believe I went to the Yugoslavs just in time. Any later and I might not have benefitted from the sound of new voices, or the rejuvenating sun, salty air and rocky ground of Krk. The beautiful Adriatic road, healing after what had happened. I learned every pothole and curve, and began, after a time, to understand the meaning of the joke Fate had played. Guillaume's lessons sank deeper into me—the impossibility of perfect love in this world, and the fact that when Love levels its forces, a mortal will is less than insignificant. During my years on the Adriatic, I felt a slow transformation of my suffering, and a hint of peace.

So the Greek, Theokopolis, found me in a state resembling rejuvenation. He bought me, shipped me to the New World, and began all those years of restoration, until his heart failed his commitment to show his wife the North American continent. And then Spencer, peddling cremation urns that day, and seeing his and Phoebe's future in my rambling lines—so I came to see that Theokopolis' plans were self-deception, that his task was only to rehabilitate me for Spencer and Phoebe, and for this, my last adventure.

It strikes me how much of the past remembers like a dream, distorted at the edges, oddly-coloured, its perspective and hours subtly altered. Places I've been, people I've carried inside of me—ones who appreciated me, others who gave me nothing—the myriad energies—

energies, because words, in any language, mean so much less than the souls that propel them. (What worlds of difference between those at whose centre Eros stirs, and those in whom he is punished with words; in the end, the last, disembodied word is a sacrilege.) The only truth is feeling.

Or rather, I should say that feeling is true, and so is the fact that we are, all of us, in the midst of undying transition. How many times, since 1938, have I fallen brittle and rusty, so they had to grind me down and weld me? How many parts have mechanics changed at every tune-up and overhaul, each removal and replacement? What gasket, pipe, cable or panel has not been changed? There is no mechanical reason I won't live, in some form, forever, but what resemblance do I bear to my original self? These deep, ambiguous changes. Who can say whether, and exactly when, I became something other than I was at birth, or when I will no longer be the Bettina in love with her scholar? For each snail advance of wisdom, I've felt a creeping setback—a compromise, despair. Phoebe has maintained me with her discerning hands, Spencer has driven me carefully, alertly. They've hung Spencer's bird cages and flower pots in me, Phoebe has tattooed blossoms on me, and the kitchen the Greek built in me, but never used, is now filled with the scent of herbs and spices. The traffic is light through me—I take only six or eight passengers. I rarely drive the same road twice. I appreciate these things. That is to say, I appreciate living with Spencer and Phoebe at this late stage. The best of people. What a gift that I might assist and guide them, be the place in which they suffer their love. If I could have one wish, it would be that they, with their pure hearts, could find their way to perfect love, and that I might be their vessel. And at another time I might have allowed myself to pretend that Guillaume's tragic vision did not apply to every true love. I might have imagined exceptions, or one exception at least—but, and here comes the sadness again, I feel an undeniable decline after all these decades, and my hope has turned fleeting. It is so clear now that within each new beginning lies an ending, curled up tightly.

Someone might argue that *Le Roman de la Rose* has a happy ending, that Guillaume's work was completed by another writer Jean de Meung, near the turn of the fourteenth century, forty years after Guillaume's death. The simple fact is, as my scholar would have put it, that Jean de Meung was a thief. My scholar actually refused to speak about de Meung's "ending" at all except to deny it. As he put it, Guillaume de Lorris was a courtly romantic, a devotee of Love, a pursuer of intangibles—how could a misogynist, bourgeois philistine like that scribbler, de Meung, possibly be his heir? de Meung transformed an elegant tale into a dull log of encyclopaedic learning, and more importantly, made love over as cruel seduction, ending his *Roman* with an obscene and unambiguous conquest in which the dreamer plucks the rose—"gather ye rosebuds while ye may," he sniggers as he buttons his trousers.

Jean de Meung, a despicable windbag, with neither insight nor subtlety. His attempt to "finish" *Le Roman* is an insult, which is why my scholar had a bookbinder make him a leather copy of Guillaume's work alone—so that he need never consider the intrusion again. Guillaume's conclusion stands: the perfect love a lover feels so near his fingertips is, at last, unattainable.

The weight of this truth, after so many centuries, presses Spencer and Phoebe to their knees. I have come to believe that they will part, that for them, there is too much baggage.

I have suffered many endings. Now I sense a final one. If I embrace my people too tightly, forgive me.

∾

Dawn. They've slept restlessly again. Spencer rises first, sweaty and irritated, tries not to wake Phoebe. His dreams have been repetitive, tediously stressful. The infection has glued his eye shut, his hand shakes as he medicates himself. He walks to the lake to bathe. The water cools the burning.

In a while Phoebe rises too. She is sombre, possessed by a dream; she fears the darkness that grows in her. She's woken this way often lately, the dream already evaporated, but still eclipsing her. The only dreams Phoebe has remembered since living with Spencer are wild ones in which she and various incubi make passionate love—she would always wake feeling bruised, flushed. But these dreams have avoided her since last autumn, about the same time Spencer's own nocturnal meetings with succubi ended, and with them, his first wet dreams since the age of fifteen.

Phoebe goes to find Spencer at the water. On a morning like this, if Spencer is heroic, he might be able to make her laugh, but the laughter will always be unbalanced, and can quickly turn to tears. Anyway, there's no heroism in Spencer this morning, and when Phoebe expresses her alarm at the sight of his eye, and insists again that he take specialized treatment, he simply tells her, irrelevantly, that the water isn't as cold as one would expect. They've both bathed and swam by the time Erika, Hallgren and Joy get up. Hallgren and Joy go down to the water, Erika sits down to breakfast with Phoebe and Spencer. Spencer has installed his eye patch. He and Phoebe are far, far away from one another. The emotions follow simple co-ordinates.

We are back on the road when everyone has eaten, and the beds are made. Not far on, at Page, we stop to take on bottled water, and to let Erika buy the new *Vogue*, due out today. In front of the Page Wal-Mart, as Spencer wheels the cases of water toward me, Hallgren and Joy run into old friends.

A parking lot in Page, Arizona. An unlikely place for New Yorkers to run across friends, though it's clear Hallgren and Joy know many people. There's a young woman named Georgia, holding the hand of a young man whose name escapes everyone immediately upon hearing it. Georgia is clearly wealthy—the silk charmeuse dress, the gold bangles; the nameless man is similarly well-heeled, but younger than Georgia, maybe nineteen, and self-conscious. (Thomas, back in the Keys, would smile and call him Georgia's boy toy.) Georgia is gentle and respectful with him.

The third person is Mary, who would be generous to a fault were generosity a fault. Phoebe, shortly after meeting her, compliments her watch, so Mary unclasps it, says, "Try it on," and when Phoebe does, says the watch looks better on Phoebe's wrist, and that she should keep it. She smiles, waves aside Phoebe's objections, says she'd be hurt if Phoebe didn't keep it. Her wrist looks naked with its band of untanned skin.

It's decided that Mary, Georgia and Georgia's gigolo are coming to Sedona with us. We go with them to a car rental outlet, and they abandon the car they've been driving. We stop at a bakery for fresh bread. Mary and Georgia browse in the jewellery store next to the bakery, and Mary turns out to be the fifty-thousandth customer to enter. Her prize is (what else?) a new watch. The delighted owner clutches her for a photograph— they'll hang her picture in the window above the rings. The new watch covers the band of white skin. She laughs: as quickly as she gives, she receives. Of course generosity begets generosity, but this *sui generis* creation of bounty is surely the miracle of her.

And now, two hours later, packed with cool water, fresh bread, we go deeper into the desert, our three extra passengers in peril of catching the psychic cross-fire between Spencer and Phoebe. For now, everyone is probably safe—Spencer drives, squinting with his good eye through half a pair of sunglasses. Phoebe sits far back of the driver's seat, to continue work on the horseshoe tattoo on Hallgren's ankle. Still, I can't help but notice how this tension resembles the ominous feeling after Phoebe's and Spencer's first and last overtly sexual episode.

Spencer had purchased me from Theokopolis' widow and was no longer staying in William's house, but rather sleeping on the futon in what would become his and Phoebe's bedroom. It happened the same night Phoebe arrived in Red Deer from Montreal, after resigning from the hospital. Afterward, they would each admit that having sex contradicted the dictates of their better judgement. As Phoebe puts it, "We had sex and started fighting. Just like that, as though a storm blew in." Spencer just calls it "the riddle."

The fall-out of the event nearly destroyed us. Phoebe said she was going back to her operating theatre, and Spencer muttered, "Fine, go!" as he settled in my driver's seat to take her to the plane. Which was when Phoebe referred to me as the damned bus.

I've been called far worse things by mechanics, who are often foul-mouthed, and sometimes entertainingly so, by bored drivers, or cramped, ungrateful passengers.

Theokopolis, even, was abusive occasionally. But these three words of Phoebe's—"the damned bus"—were the worst of all. In the three days I'd had with Spencer, and the hours with Phoebe, I'd let my hopes go very high. All I wanted was to make them happy, and suddenly they were at one another's throats, and now this.

I wanted them to scrap me then and there. So, of course, when Spencer turned my key, I seized. I couldn't even turn over. And then Spencer was chasing Phoebe out my front door, and into the quiet Red Deer street, catching up with her far down the street. Both of them shouting. Then, both consoling. They seemed a bit better when they returned. The seizing was a damp distributor.

But the phantoms unleashed in an hour on a futon! Gods jostling with one another for status and recognition, or wanting to be placated. Beginning their long, unelaborated haunting. It's remarkable, really, how I could have been so sensitive at my age, after so many hundreds of thousands of kilometres—how a few rabble-rousing members of Spencer and Phoebe's crowded souls could kick me into submission. When they finally forgave one another their forwardness, I began to relax, but the pain of the memory still overtakes me on a day like this. Today I feel like I'm running on seven cylinders.

I feel tired, hopeless, overheated. I need a rest, so I create one. I wait until we approach a gentle curve, and undo my clutch cable. When Spencer touches my clutch, it falls to the floor. We stop.

∿

I expect we'll be here a couple of hours. Repairing my clutch will take Phoebe ten minutes, but then they'll have lunch. At Page, generous Mary bought wine, patés, smoked salmon, and strawberries, so it will be a pleasant picnic. (Also, at the newsstand, when Erika picked out her copy of the new *Vogue*, Mary bought every other fashion magazine in stock for her—ones from Rome, Paris, London. Erika is in Heaven.) Phoebe skitters underneath me to reattach my clutch cable.

It feels good to have Phoebe's hands on me, and to have her talk only to me. There has not been enough of this. When she works on me, she tells me she loves my ancient configurations, my old, clumsily cast parts. She makes jokes that only the two of us understand.

Once, in Vermont, as she changed a gasket, she said that new vehicles ought to be a contravention of international law. The foolish Modern, she said, rushes her late model to the repair shop when an umbrella punctures the headliner, and finds a door ding cause for a nervous breakdown. Perfectionism resents ageing, she said, fears it. Which caused her to speculate about when I would have passed from being a new bus to being an old one. Was it a certain pot-hole I went through, or an upholstery burn? And then she said the most beautiful thing: that people had to choose between replacing their possessions weekly, and revelling in the ageing. She called me "excellent in my dotage."

Her attention makes me beautiful. I am honoured to be her confidante. She manipulates my many parts, prays with me, confesses. One day, not far from Carmel— she called it Caramel; I love it when she muddles her words—she was feeling blue, and she whispered to me, "Medicine, like mechanics, is helpless in the face of fragility," and then she stood still for a while, astonished at how close to the edge we all stood. She said it was a wonder human infants weren't fitted with portable heart-lung machines at birth, in advance of the heart attacks that could come later in life. It is a fact that before she decided on medicine, she toyed with becoming a nun. She calls religion "medicine for the soul," and she has whispered to me, "When you are born, your death is born with you. And what is a doctor anyway, if not a gentle priest who decorates your small ceremonies, and holds your hand as you die?" A lovely thought, and how gentle her hands are. Probably all I really needed today was a dose of her full attention. I feel so much better by the time she's done and has slipped out from under me, joining the others for lunch.

After lunch, Hallgren insists on a group photo as a memento of the unbearable heat. When Spencer volunteers to snap it, Phoebe complains he's such a slow photographer that everyone will have sunstroke before he finishes. But it's all right. Hallgren sets the camera on a chair and uses the self-timer. Then he and Joy go off into the rocks with their blanket, a bottle of water, a bucket of ice, and a bag of cherries. They'll strip down and cover up with sun-blocking creams. Georgia and her man-without-a-name try flying a kite in the desert wind.

Spencer and Phoebe go walking, but not together. Phoebe and Erika go east. In twenty-four hours, they've become the dearest of friends. Phoebe's wide straw hat blows off her head and tumbles like a weed across the sand. Erika catches it, ties it back onto Phoebe. Spencer goes the other direction, enclosed in his drug- and pain-altered consciousness, and frets about Erika and Phoebe becoming lovers.

The sun is past its apex when he climbs back through my door, and gulps a litre of water from the cooler. He's lost fluid to both perspiration and tears. Over the whir of the big fan, he can make out the low sound of Georgia and her man, X, talking dirty. Hallgren and Joy return from their tanning, flushed and ruddy, smelling of coconut. They are laughing, their mouths bright red from feeding one another cherries without using their hands. Spencer is about to sit in the driver's seat and honk my horn to make Phoebe and Erika come back, but they arrive on their own just then. Erika occupies the conversational space; Phoebe is in no condition. Phoebe balances at the edge of a sadness as yawning as any of the canyons the ground around here opens into. Under cover of Erika's gregariousness, she avoids Spencer, and makes her way to her tattooing pens.

Spencer at the front of me, Phoebe moving to the back. An emotional sniper's alley. Spencer turns my key. Phoebe sits down in her tattooing chair.

Hallgren goes to Phoebe to receive the other half of his horseshoe.

∾

Twenty months ago we set out. The geese had left Red Deer, and we'd passed our last nights without frost. Winter was descending. South seemed the obvious direction.

I'd been given a splendid make-over. Phoebe had stencilled a border of flowers around the top of my inside walls, painted blossoms on my outside, and fastened pots full of real plants to my floor—cacti, jades, a fig (and the columbine, clematis and peonies, which Phoebe consistently confused with concubine, chlamydia and penises)—they hung Spencer's old bird cages with their budgies and cockatiels. They reupholstered the Greek's old easy chairs, and bought futons for the berths and curtains to mark off the sleeping compartments. Spencer stowed his old sixteen-millimetre projector into my hold, with canisters full of forgotten comedies, and hid the portable television down there as well—only recently has the TV come out. They installed a fine stereo and many little speakers, installed the telephone and computer. It was William who suggested installing the fax-modem into the computer. He was the one who thought of faxing ahead to hostels, or university travel offices, in cities we seemed aimed toward, advertising our likeliest destinations, offering flexible ride-sharing. William said that faxing ahead, plus Internet word-of-mouth, was good business.

Finally, they stocked my kitchen, and I was on the road, approaching the speed limit at times, stretching myself for the first time since Yugoslavia, blowing the carbon out of my system, feeling good after the immobile years on Theokopolis' property.

In retrospect, it seems that we were headed for Southern Florida, but we did not know that at the time. We found riders from ride boards, through telephone calls and fax conversations, wandering in cyberspace. We accepted passengers whose destinations interested us, referred others on, and sometimes travelled without passengers, aimed ourselves instead at, say, a town or city said to have an old movie house with velvet seats, heavy curtains, gilt walls. Sometimes we simply liked the sound of a place name—Lovelock...Matador...Pensacola—or got side-tracked in natural wonders—Spencer, newly in love with fly-fishing, needed to remain in Northern Michigan, and two passengers, in a hurry to make Chicago, had to transfer to a Greyhound.

"Great run!" you'd hear Spencer or Phoebe say after a day's drive.

"You said it!" the other would reply, laughing. "Just think if we had passengers..."

The turmoil surrounding their first carnal encounter had abated. The ghosts had left the stage, gone to the wings to await their next cues. Phoebe and Spencer mostly got along well. She called him a neat freak; no doubt, in tidiness, she was the more relaxed one. And her palms perspired when he raced me over eighty kilometres per hour. "Slow down, Spencer," she'd say, and tap his knee, "We're starting to shake. Slow down!" And sometimes it annoyed her when he stopped to pee in meadows, and on trees at the side of the road. He sipped water from a thermos as he drove, several litres a day. She thought he should use the on-board bathroom to pee. He said he liked the fresh air.

Evenings, unless they were rushing a passenger somewhere, they went for a long walk. Afterward, Spencer might work at his computer, while Phoebe played flute for the plants, visited with the birds, made prank calls to radio talk shows. If there were passengers, Spencer would bake tea biscuits for morning. And then they stepped behind the partition that marked off their little bedroom, slid into bed together, and read aloud to one another from thick novels. This is not to suggest that they avoided the subject of sex—though this would have been understandable, given what had happened their first night in Red Deer—only that they had mutually, if tacitly, accepted certain physical boundaries in bed. In fact, they talked about their abstinence quite often.

Actually, Phoebe and William talked about sex most—William, it seemed, loved nothing more than a good fax or phone rap about celibacy. That is, he acknowledged the centrality of sex in the average, successful life, and admitted that for the wrong person, celibacy would be a psycho-spiritual catastrophe. That said, he had himself abstained from sex for three years, and not because training for the ministry compelled him to—it didn't—but because he judged his past sexual affairs to have been a distraction from the life he wanted to lead. True, he was an incurable flirt, but, for him, sex was a monumental waste of energy. Phoebe agreed sex was a distraction, even if, like Spencer, she had to admit that the sex she and Spencer had had that evening in Red Deer had been outstanding, objectively speaking.

She and William swapped theories about the origin of the terrible discord. Phoebe called William's explanations obscure—for example, that Spencer and Phoebe had projected every negative image of relationships onto the carnal act that day—and William found Phoebe's sociological and historical thoughts superficial. They faxed notes to one another about stress, the calamitous conjunction of moons and stars over Red Deer that day, about Spencer's upbringing, and Phoebe's penchant for laproscopic surgery. Phoebe found the discussion with William stimulating, and there was the fact that William, something of an authority on scandals involving late-mediaeval and early Renaissance priests, could compose a very bawdy fax.

Mostly, these discussions irritated Spencer. After all, it was he, far more than Phoebe, who, after the light was turned out at the end of a long day, would drift toward sleep, only to have his hypnogogia invaded by wildly erotic images, and find himself pacing, wide awake, outside. There were private faxes between him and William—male moments, Phoebe called them—in the course of which William told Spencer baldly that from everything he knew, the life Spencer was living with Phoebe was nothing short of cowardice.

∾

Twenty months. It feels both like twenty years and twenty minutes since we started. Love was, then as now, the only topic that mattered. All conversation orbited it. All activity sanctified it.

They let the birds out of their cages so they flew on the current of the music from the stereo. They played backgammon, engaged in conversations hours long, read to one another as I filled with the scent of Spencer's baking tea biscuits, or one of Phoebe's basil-infused stews. They gave one another flowers and chocolate, or gifts of fruit— a trio of perfect plums in a swatch of red cloth, fresh peaches or pears, a basket of wild cherries or mulberries; pomegranate, fruit that grew from the blood of Dionysus.

Love.

So many, many people we carried, for short distances—from town to town in a morning—or for journeys days long. Pleasant, boring, and rude people, the affectionate and callous, the dull and the brilliant. The subject of love was always current, even in the mouths of the erotically slothful, though their lexicons of love were poverty-stricken, though Eros had long sat in their hide-out-souls, in a straight-backed chair, gagged and bound. What variety we saw.

Withdrawn and passive ones, polite throughout the few banal contacts they'd suffered, who lived unaware of desire beyond a twice-weekly or twice-annual in-and-out, and who fled from magic, resorting in the most desperate moments to Reason, that biggest of all pains. Or the ones who claimed love wasn't worth speaking about, but whose insides were overgrown by it, in a twisted and tangled underbrush that would have turned back the most fearless explorer. Saccharine girlfriends who thought love was coffee sweetener, and whose thoughts were most stirred by the romantic fantasies of glossy magazines; or the serious studs more bent on conquest than love, who lent their hearts instead of giving them, whose footsteps scorched the earth. Or the young couples who read *Laughable Loves* aloud, explored the various combative roles, and others, flipsides of these Kundera couples— educated, usually white—who said all sex was exploitation. One man argued at length, continually checking his lover for approval, that as a man, he was a rapist, basically.

Though there were others, from time to time, who gave hearing to, and seemed to explore their instincts. Incidental sex, like the swells of more or less competently-played music behind Phoebe and Spencer, the more or less unwitting players. Some, granted, who honoured athleticism more than love, or saw love as a commodity to be collected like new shoes. Some who didn't enjoy it much, apart from the thrill, some who loved absently, many who simply loved. But everything was possible within me, and, as stories about us leaked into the collective travel lore, it felt as though the occasions of creativity increased.

This was life. Many made love within me. Naked, nearly naked bodies, pulsing, sucking, moaning. Couplings, under cover of darkness, on the rocking of the highway, as Phoebe and Spencer sat up front over cups of tea, deep in conversation, my dashboard lights illuming their faces. Or in the depths of the night as they slept, or would have slept if they could have…

So, the overtly sexual life, though Spencer and Phoebe denied it to themselves, was nonetheless a nexus in their thoughts, not in a vulgar way, but with gravity, a certain solemnity. Without discussing it, they began to give one another more provocative things: lingerie, teddies for her, silk boxers, clip-on nipple rings for him. And late one evening, after Spencer screened one of his old black and white movies, they managed to laugh together for the first time about their abstinence.

It was Big Sur. They'd brought six UCLA literature students up from L.A. to visit Henry Miller's house, an erotically-charged place because of its late occupant. They'd projected the film onto the white wall of a campground washroom building, and then the students had gone off in search of a drink. It was Phoebe's turn to wash the dishes, though the film and the hours of sea air had made her sleepy. She asked Spencer if he would consider doing them, and when, predictably, he refused, she offered the unthinkable. "Come on, Spence," she said. "Look, I'll give you a blow-job." Absurd. They did the dishes together, and they laughed and laughed and laughed.

∾

A trio stands out when I think back on everyone we've met these past twenty months. Three people who, in their own ways, inadvertently served Fate's grand design to widen the chasm between Spencer and Phoebe.

A chain of three links: Bernadette, Josie, Thomas.

We picked Bernadette up in Austin, Texas, where she said she'd been working in a florist's shop, making 8-millimetre documentaries about erotic themes in film, and planning a documentary feature along the same lines, what she described as "kind of a pornographic *That's Entertainment.*" Though when we met her, she was beginning "an erotic exploration of America," and she rode a circuitous route with us through Oklahoma, southern Kansas, Missouri, Arkansas, finally leaving us in Morgan City, Louisiana, a short jog from where she'd started. "I have a sneaking suspicion," she said one morning in Kansas over coffee and toast, "that when it comes to porn, normal America is an incredibly freaky place."

Nearly every moment Bernadette travelled, she kept one eye to her camcorder viewfinder. She videotaped scenery and buildings as we drove, and when we stopped in cities or towns, she engaged people in cafés and stores, on college campuses, in churches after service, tunnelling deeply and with remarkable speed into their lives. She accessed the fantasies of women and men, partnered or single, gay or straight—their secrets, their every pornographic proclivity, and occasionally—as if she worked by mesmerism—she was invited into their living rooms and bedrooms to videotape erotic magazine and video collections, and collections of erotic bric-à-brac. She recorded notes for narration onto micro-cassettes, sketched images and scenarios into blue notebooks. She worked long days, but claimed she did her best writing in bed, especially from dreams, which she complained evaporated too quickly on waking. A week after she came aboard, she woke in the middle of the night in her berth, and made a series of sketches in felt marker on the white sheet covering her. In the morning she copied the notes to paper, but of course the sheet was ruined.

The incident with the sheet might have irritated Phoebe and Spencer had the culprit been anyone else, but something about Bernadette captivated them, so they prized the damaged sheet. Maybe the way her eyes opened so wide when she recounted something that had shocked her—very little shocked her, and when something did, it rarely shocked anyone else—or her odd inquisitiveness, what Phoebe described to William as "a blend of worldliness, aplomb, and an almost spiritual naiveté." Maybe what fascinated Spencer and Phoebe about Bernadette was the fact that it never occurred to her to justify what she was doing.

Neither sociologist nor activist, Bernadette was simply a documentary artist, watching, recording, assembling. "Number one," she said, "erotica is like water: you need it even if you don't know why—people will always need explicit images of sex. Number two, there's good porn and bad porn, and if there's any justice in the world, some day people will be able to see good." Maybe she was part anthropologist, the way she sat over one of her notebooks at breakfast, and noted that, for example, while most men fancied skin mags, flicks, and strippers, and liked to explore them alone, women, on the whole, preferred reading John Donne or Anaïs Nin, and liked to share their porn with a friend. Or, as she said after taping late into the night at a private piercing and flaying party in St. Louis, at which a local performance artist performed the old trick of nailing his scrotum to a board, "People in sexual subcultures appreciate erotica far more than the average liberal hetero. For the people at that party, a good image is just everything. Bettina runs on gasoline—a sexual subculture runs on sexual images."

And then, near the end of our time together, she videotaped first Spencer, and then Phoebe, sitting at the computer. Later that day, when Spencer and Phoebe returned from a walk, they overheard Bernadette dictating the following scenario onto her microcassette: "A man and woman each log onto several erotic billboards on the sly. For several weeks they explore chat and match-making lines, read text files and stories, settle on a particular billboard, and in another week begin a cyberspace affair with another person. In one more week, they arrange meetings with their respective billboard paramours, make excuses to be out of the house, end up meeting one another, and having the best dates, and the best sex, of their lives…"

Spencer and Phoebe stepped inside then, both offended, disturbed. Bernadette winked at them, concluded, "Simultaneous cheating, betrayal-in-common, etc.," and clicked the Stop button. "Did you hear?" she said. "What did you think?"

If they had been questioned, neither Spencer nor Phoebe would have been able to explain why they remained silent, or even why they felt victimized—maybe Bernadette's story felt to each of them vaguely like the betrayal of a confidence. In any case, the calm between them turned stormy, and, later that night, as if they had forgotten Bernadette was still there, they fought.

"It's so damned typical," Phoebe said. "Men slinking around behind the little woman's back...!"

And Spencer, "As if women don't do the same damned thing?"

"Isn't one solid relationship enough for a guy? What does a man want from a woman anyway?"

Bernadette said nothing, but pressed her Sony's "Record" button. She toyed with the idea of picking her camcorder up off of the chair.

"What does a man want?" Spencer said. "Just someone to talk to. Intelligence, a bit of humour, honesty..."

"I see. Is that all?"

Spencer thought. "Well, now that you mention it, I guess most men would want someone to share a bit of bodily warmth with..."

Phoebe made a face. "Yes, well, there it is. That's what a man wants in a woman: a splendid fuck, nice tits and a tight little ass."

"No! No more than a woman has to have a guy with a ten inch dong…"

They were too involved in their argument to notice that Bernadette had set her camera zoom to the widest angle, placed the camera on the table, aimed at them.

Phoebe was saying, "God, Spencer, why would anyone inject sex into a perfectly good relationship?"

Spencer said, "Well, just for the sake of the argument, why wouldn't they?"

"Because it's just so damned desperate, Spencer."

"Desperate."

"Yes, desperate. The whole idea behind sex is the continuation of the species. Can you get anymore desperate than that?"

"The continuation of the species? How about sex completing two peoples' love for one another? Like Aristophanes says in Plato's *Sympos…*"

Phoebe shook her head. "Don't, Spencer. Don't get in over your head. I mean, you're no William…"

"How dare you! You can be such an asshole!"

Phoebe sighed. "Okay, say we start boinking…"

Spencer, incensed. "What say we *don't?*"

"If your goal is normalcy, we might as well get married too. Voilà: economic, legal, religious shackles, and our sex life really dies. We're better off the way we are."

A snort. "Sexual *in our own way...*"

"Right, and what's the matter with that?"

"What's the matter with it? It's unnatural, that's what's the matter with it."

She dismissed this with a wave of her hand.

"You just don't like my body," he said.

She rolled her eyes. "They should give your body an Academy Award..."

"I'm serious, Phoebe. You don't like my body."

"Of course I do. Your shoulders and chest are to die for."

"My shoulders and chest? What are those but things anyone on a beach can see?"

"Oh, what's the matter with you? I love your stomach too, and you have a wonderful ass. Your cock is just about the loveliest I've ever seen."

Now he rolled his eyes.

"Whatever is your point? We're just not like that. Sex isn't important. I mean, it's not like you masturbate or something..."

"Phoebe, of course I do!"

"You do?"

"I'll get prostate cancer if I don't. You think I want prostate cancer?"

"You masturbate? That's so gross!"

They heard Bernadette stifle a laugh, and realized the exchange was being videotaped.

Spencer said, "Bernadette, I'd rather you turned the camera off…"

Phoebe said, "Why, Spence? Don't want anyone to know you masturbate?"

"Actually, it has nothing to do with masturbation…"

Phoebe said, "Spencer, the issue is the combination of sex and love. Why do you think we turned so cranky the day we screwed?"

"Well, I don't know. It's not like the sex was terrible."

"The sex was fine."

"Just fine. I see." Apparently, he had forgotten about the camera.

"Oh, don't go and get all hurt. We got cranky because sex plus companionship equals cranky. We've been fine since we stopped having sex."

"Phoebe, your math is stupid. I mean, what, companionship minus sex always equals some kind of placid togetherness?"

"Really, I guess that would be *flaccid* togetherness," Bernadette said from behind the camera.

Phoebe laughed.

"Sorry, Spencer," Bernadette said. "I couldn't resist that."

Spencer said, "Phoebe, your basic problem is you don't understand men. You think we're all a bunch of stiff-membered, dirty-minded creeps."

"Is that so?"

"Yes, in my estimation. You think sex is dirty. You think male desires are basically vile."

"Not all men's de…"

"Has it ever occurred to you that as an instinct, lust might not be so much vile and base, as merely primal? You know, Phoebe, natural, healthy, normal…"

"Oh, well, thank you for the interpretation, Herr Doktor."

"Don't do that. I hate it when you do that…"

"Hey, man, did you take some kind of pill to make you so goddamned smart?" Phoebe's face retained its laugh lines, but her eyes were very serious. "Spencer, abstinence is our only hope."

When she said it, the meaning was clearer to him than it had ever been before. "Think about it," she said.

It was a door closing.

∾

Bernadette left us a few days later. She'd planned to come with us to New Orleans, but met a gas jockey in Morgan City, and told us to go on ahead. I recall sitting at the edge of a bayou the evening of the day she left us. Spencer and Phoebe were eating dinner, going over things Bernadette had told them about the mysterious swamp life of the south. The water snakes swam close to where I was parked, as if they'd gladly come up and lie under my tires. I recalled gophers I'd run over—and possums, dogs, the few deer, a surprising number of snakes. Never a crocodile. My tires had never been near one of those.

Passengers had come and gone. Somehow Bernadette had been more than all the others, and now everything felt too quiet. Bernadette had wanted to see a crocodile.

∾

When we picked Josie up the very next day in Mississippi, we wished Bernadette was still with us. Bernadette would have loved Josie.

Josephine Alexandra Meredith, with the lightest blonde hair, fair-skinned, with freckles that doubled at the slightest hint of sunlight. Thin, even unhealthily so, though a certain raspiness in her bearing almost filled her out. Josie worked a ring and milk-bottle game on a carnival midway. Sometimes, on the side, she turned tricks with locals—she was saving money for something that was a secret, and she called hooking her exercise.

When we met her, she was with four other carnies at a Biloxi service station. They'd been driving to the next show in Greenville, and their car had broken down between Gulfport and Biloxi. There'd been some trouble diagnosing the problem, and a wait for parts. The owner of the car had to stay in Biloxi, but Josie and the three others jumped at our offer to take them on to Greenville.

Biloxi to Greenville, three hundred and fifty kilometres, and a graduate seminar in vice. No sooner were we on the road than the two men and the woman, whom we had initially mistaken for a repulsive little man, encircled the kitchen table and started in on boilermakers and a five-card draw spree with all the cursing, jostling, accusations and cheating of a roller derby. When Spencer and Phoebe weren't looking, the carnies consumed a fascinating and extensive array of drugs.

Josie sat apart from the others. She leaned back in an easy chair and read a mystery novel, until Phoebe joined her. This was before Phoebe learned tattooing. Phoebe asked her about her tattoos, and Josie was happy to tell the story of each one. Then she demonstrated the proper technique for stretching skin under tattoo needles, and re-told stories she'd heard of men having their penises tattooed, and masochists hitting the tattoo shop on a Friday afternoon for a dry run—all the needles, none of the ink. She shook her head and said, "Men, they're just so…" and laughed with Phoebe.

Up at the wheel, Spencer's aural attentions lay fragmented. A line from the song on the stereo, now a roar of a curse from the card table, now something Josie was saying. He turned off the music and tried to zoom in close on Phoebe and Josie.

Josie was dividing the human race into two groups: one with dicks, and one without. The group attached to dicks communicated in grunts, were basically animal in nature. The other group had soft bodies, capable of giving and receiving love. Phoebe didn't know whether Josie was serious. She said, "Some men are really all right. Some men know a lot."

Josie shook her head. "A man wouldn't know something erotic from a hole in the ground."

"As it were," Phoebe laughed.

Josie said, "For a man, everything's wrapped up in the tiny projection of his body that he needs to harden and empty out."

Tiny, Spencer thought. He was glad to be out of the conversation.

Josie said, "It's this uncontrollable thing for them. They're like robots. They'll lie, plead, beg and argue to get you in the sack or the back seat of their car. They'll make complete fools of themselves. Then, once you go with them, you realize you might as well not be there. It's just a workout for them. They're a bunch of athletes with crazy expectations…"

One card player began cursing another violently, and, without thinking, Spencer pushed down a bit on my gas pedal. He felt jangled, uneasy—the card players, Josie—though listening to Josie was a mixed experience, and her words acted in him like a sort of charm. Tense and calm at once—the contradictory desires of a soul. He let up on my pedal.

Josie said, "Want to know the average man's two greatest fantasies? First, a one-nighter with a teen-aged virgin who speaks no English. Second, fucking with the sexiest woman alive, namely himself in drag, because they're narcissists, every one of them. The men around here are a sorry bunch. I've read that they laugh at our men over in India. They say the men are different in India."

"Maybe an Indian man would make a good lover."

Josie smiled. "Maybe, though I can't see myself bothering. There are enough women around you don't need to."

Josie held Phoebe's eyes. "Anyway, a woman's body is way better than a man's. Two women making love understand one another. It's an incredible feeling. You and I know something a man can never know, and there's a desire that just goes on and on. It's bottomless. We're never satisfied."

Phoebe wanted to look away, and Spencer wondered if the feeling of raw anxiety in him might also be bottomless.

Though the anxiety he felt right then was nothing compared with what he felt when the big man in the green cowboy shirt started making indecent suggestions to Josie. Strange how this guy had been the quietest one at the card table. Suddenly he wanted to give Josie the rest of the cash he had on the table for an hour on one of the futons. Josie just flipped him the finger over her shoulder and kept talking to Phoebe, until the guy started to say exactly how much money he wanted to pay, and specifically what he wanted in exchange for it. Then he reached into his duffle bag, drew out a tattered skin magazine, and opened it to a black and white photo spread of Josie at a younger age.

Now she turned around. "Ivan, when are you ever going to get tired of that?" she said. "And when are you going to get it through that ugly skull of yours that I only work for humans?"

And at this, he started calling Josie names, and stood up unsteadily, but menacingly, and Spencer felt a vast, swollen anger. Phoebe shouted that she wanted the man to leave the bus. Spencer agreed, but wanted him off at that exact moment, so he hit my brakes hard to throw the guy off balance, simultaneously kicked my emergency brake, opened my door, and picked up the big crescent wrench beside his seat. He was out of his seat well before I'd come to a stop.

And then he was standing over the drugged, drunken man, holding the wrench over his head and ordering him to keep his hands where everyone could see them as he nudged him out my front door with the toe of his boot. The others at the card table seemed to like it when Phoebe tossed the duffle bag out, and it hit him in the shoulder. She gave the magazine to Josie.

Spencer took his seat, pulled the brake, and put me in first gear. The remaining card players dealt a new hand and opened new beers. Far behind us, on the shoulder of the road, the man staggered to his feet and waved a fist in the air.

"That was fun," Josie said, though as she said it, she was already leafing through the magazine, and drifting on old thoughts. After a while, she said, "I was fat back then, wasn't I?" and showed Phoebe the photographs. Phoebe didn't answer, because the woman on the page was waif-like.

We stopped behind a grove of evergreen trees at a turn-out thirty kilometres later. Phoebe made left-over fried chicken sandwiches for everyone. She made Spencer's with sliced Harvard beets the way he liked them, then went off to eat lunch on a blanket with Josie, at the edge of a farmer's field. Spencer stayed behind to guard me against the card players, who were skipping lunch in favour of more alcohol. The sight of Phoebe off in the distance, cross-legged, sketching something in ball-point onto Josie's arm, left him uneasy, though it wasn't until we were back on the road, and the card players had passed out, that his anxiety turned acute. Josie lounged on the futon nearest the easy chairs, and told Phoebe she felt more relaxed than she had in weeks. She stretched, and Phoebe said the stretch looked like it had felt good, and Josie smiled, said, "I learned to stretch from my cat." The way Phoebe smiled made Spencer think she was falling in love.

∾

After the day with Josie, Phoebe read everything she could find about tattoos, though she didn't actually begin tattooing for several months, until a passenger, Jesus de Jesus, riding with us from Augusta, agreed to sell her the tattooing guns he had at home in Jacksonville.

At first, she practised on uncooked chickens, then graduated to giving Spencer a small maple leaf on the left side of his belly. "The most surgically-clean tattoos in America," she boasted as she hung her medical diplomas on the wall, beside a powerful, overhead light. It was thus that Phoebe crossed her medical and artistic talents.

Spencer liked seeing her so happy, though every time he saw her engrossed in some magazine or book about tattoos, each time she showed him some new design she'd sketched, and as she began to take clients, he always thought of Josie, milk-blonde bottle and rings administrator and prostitute, and how she had learned to stretch from her cat.

∾

Eventually, we arrived in southern Florida. Spencer and Phoebe spent a bit of time lying in the sun, but more time working—taking tourists down the Keys, through the Everglades, up and down the coast. Phoebe developed her tattoo skills, and Spencer spent hours at the computer. In all, we stayed just over eleven months. I recall it as a time of great activity, an elaborate busy-ness, almost a crowdedness.

We met Thomas in Florida. A sweet Englishman, though he could also be wicked. A defrocked priest of the Roman Catholic Church, avid comic book reader and impressionist, and now, owner of a charter boat, christened

Holy Mother, which took tourists fishing or sight-seeing. Like Robert Shaw in *Jaws*, he said, though in his middle thirties, and not his fifties.

He dropped over one night in November, after bringing a charter group back from a day of fishing for grouper and benito and marlin. It had been a hard day. His passengers had begun to sing intoxicatedly in mid-afternoon—loudly, dully as only the drunk can sing— not stopping for breaks. Even hours later, blind-pissed, hoarse, close to shore, they had begged him to head back out to open water. "One more time!" they shouted, even as he tied up the Holy Mother.

"You have given me the worst headache of my life," we heard him shout through a loud-hailer. "If you are standing on that foredeck in thirty seconds, I'll have the harbour police arrest you for trespassing, which in a maritime context, is a rather serious offence known as piracy. Do not fall into the water as you make your way onto the pier. I will not fish you out."

Spencer and Phoebe had had a full day themselves, touring a family through the Everglades. They were drinking red wine and playing backgammon when Thomas knocked on my door.

They gave him aspirin, poured him some wine, and he mewled about his day until his headache receded. By midnight, the mood had turned robust—talk had arrived, inevitably, via many tangents, at love. Now they poured a second bottle of wine into the conversation. It wouldn't be long before they opened a third.

Thomas talked about being a priest, and how troubling his vow of chastity had been. Though he'd loved his work and felt a genuine calling, he'd considered chastity to be, "a castration of humanity," unless it was used, say, in preparation for a fertility festival or orgy.

He said, having brightened significantly since the loud-hailer incident, "It's amazing to me that of all the world's religions, only Judeo-Christian ones teach us to hate sex. They want us to believe that sex ought to be about as pleasurable as cleaning fish—so of course you feel damned guilty when you actually happen to like it—and that the path to Heaven starts with abhorring the world, despising the female." He droned, "The lust of the flesh, the pride of life; none of this is of the Father, blah blah blah. The Devil, blah blah, is a woman, blah…

"Crap, every word," Thomas sermonized, "though no devout Christian from the most rosy, folk-singing congregation can imagine that sex is Divine, that it might be a preview of Heaven and not of Hell. Seems to me that Christianity came along and gave Eros poison to drink—problem is, it didn't kill him, but only turned him into this historically odd, degenerate flasher. Just to think about the millions of missionaries over the centuries infecting the world with their sexual fear and loathing makes my head ache again. Jesus himself probably wasn't the puritan the Church makes Him out to be. I swear that for two thousand years, Jesus Christ has been up in Heaven puking."

Spencer poured more wine. There'd been no word from William in a while. Maybe, after the time with Bernadette and Josie, speaking aloud about chastity again was a relief.

But chastity had only been a pit-stop in the conversation, which moved swiftly on to the subject of erotic fantasies. They brainstormed a catalogue of fantasies: sex in public places and group sex, various threesomes, brands of voyeurism.

"Confession is a turn-on," Spencer said.

Thomas feigned a swoon. "Confession!" he said. "Please don't get me started on the confessional."

"Blow-jobs are a turnoff," Phoebe said, and when she saw that Spencer and Thomas were going to disagree, she added, "Unless you're a man, in which case you probably like them so much you even fantasize about giving them."

Spencer said he didn't. Thomas said Spencer didn't know what he was missing. Spencer said the image of giving a blow-job did nothing for him, though tricking someone into sex was different.

Phoebe was appalled. "Conning someone, Spencer? Oh, Spencer!"

Thomas laughed. He had a lovely, clear laugh. "That's just so pagan, Spencer," he said. "Half of the Greek myths are about one person tricking another into bed."

And then he said, "My greatest fantasy was getting a Prince Albert...until I got one."

"You have one?" Phoebe cried. "Do you really?"

In her work with tattoos, Phoebe had learned a lot about body piercing, but she'd never met a man who'd had a ring put through the hole of his penis and out the side.

"May I see it?" she said, without thinking.

"Phoebe, Jesus!" Spencer said.

But Thomas didn't mind. He stood and unzipped his trousers. Slipped himself out of his underwear.

Phoebe and Spencer gazed at Thomas' pierced penis with its shiny gold hoop. Phoebe examined it as she would the body of a patient, and as she looked, she asked her questions. Was it true that a Prince Albert increased pleasure for both partners during sex? (Yes, Thomas said.) Had there been a religious motivation for having it done? (Yes, it was adornment to the glory of God.) And then, her examination was over. "I think it's just terrific," she told Thomas. "It's been done very well."

As Thomas put himself back in his trousers, she wondered aloud about performing a few piercings herself, then glanced at Spencer.

Spencer had been marvelling at her doctor-like distance, the way she could ask about the sexual pleasure attendant to a man's wearing a hoop in his prick, when she rejected the idea of having sex herself. And it occurred to him that he and Phoebe had been discussing fantasies they would never act on with one another. And now, here she was, wanting to try "a few piercings" herself. He glanced down at his crotch, then back at her, and spoke evenly, carefully. "Forget it," he said.

"Trust me. I'm a surgeon," she said, in strict denial of the seriousness of his statement, and held her right hand out and made it tremble.

∾

Later, Thomas told the story of how he had come to be defrocked, the vestryman, Fricks, surprising Thomas and a certain youthful seminarian, Cecil, in an intimate embrace. "I don't hold anything against Fricks," Thomas said. "Two hundred years old, father of four apparently straight boys, grandfather to a dozen more, one of the Knights of goddamned Columbus. A decent man, a good Catholic. Imagine the poor man stumbling in on his priest and another man with their tongues down one another's throats! Anything but going straight to the bishop would have been absurd.

"Fricks turned on his heel and walked out of my office, and poor Cecil chased after him, begging for his silence. I sat down in my reading chair, and took a few deep breaths. My bishop had actually known about the affair for several months, but I knew he'd *have* to begin proceedings once the enraged Mr. Fricks visited him. I experienced three waves of a horror from which I thought I might die. A remarkable horror. So I kept up my deep breathing, and focused on planting my feet firmly on the floor. I became literal, and took off my shoes and socks so I'd have fuller contact with the hardwood.

"It suddenly occurred to me then that I could still taste Cecil's kiss—he'd been sucking on a peppermint. Then it occurred to me that I was remarkably horny, astoundingly so, and that what I really wanted right now was to take my dear Cec straight to bed. And within three or four minutes, I felt the most astonishing peace—a beatific sense. I was more perfectly blessed at that moment than ever before in my life. Since childhood, I'd wanted to be a priest, and from late adolescence, I'd known that, erotically-speaking, I was worlds away from the priesthood. I see now that I'd been waiting for someone like Mr. Fricks to come along and play his part for a long time. Finally, Cecil came back to my office weeping. He told me the light behind me was shining onto my head, giving me a halo."

When Thomas had gone home to the Holy Mother, and Spencer and Phoebe were in bed with the light out, they held each other very tightly, almost ferociously, in the way that people who are lonely will do.

∽

We were in Florida until Christmas, when a group of thirty-three skiers between the ages of nineteen and twenty-two from the University of Alabama at Tuscaloosa engaged us to take them to Utah on the twenty-sixth. The run would make us financially solvent for several months, and since Phoebe and Spencer were growing restless, they said they'd take the students to Utah but not bring them back. The students agreed.

So we were covering ground again—Florida to Alabama, then on, for many hours to Utah. In more crowded quarters than we were used to, though the crush had no effect on our passengers' enthusiasm. Spencer had discovered that engine noise scrambled incoming faxes, so when he heard the code William used to say he was about to transmit—two single rings on the phone—he pulled over and stopped, shut off my motor. Before the fax paper was out of the machine, the stereo speakers had been pointed out my windows, the music had been turned up, and there were thirty-three kids dancing at the side of the Texas road. A sock-hop, Phoebe called it later, and they laughed at the word.

The Utah run, a mysterious encounter with youth. That night, a time for wondering about time that had passed, a moment of strange urgency. A couple of hours before dawn, Spencer and Phoebe woke simultaneously, and found themselves surveying the young men and women, asleep in their blankets or bags, alone or in pairs, their skis below them in my holds and their knapsacks in the racks beside them. Packs full of impractically-large clothing, economy boxes of condoms.

Spencer and Phoebe, only ten years their senior, felt a sudden longing, as if some pure, uncomplicated energy emanated from the young, sleeping bodies. They felt vaguely resentful, and then acutely so; they relived the crumminess of a seventies upbringing, felt memories of wrong turns, real and imagined, of years' worth of wasted time. But neither one said a word. Spencer slipped into his jeans and shirt, tip-toed a path through the students, took his place behind the wheel. Phoebe drew the curtain back around the futon, pulled the covers up over her head, and wished the gentle movement, as Spencer led me off the side-road and back to the highway, could help her back to sleep.

∾

A blizzard stopped us thirty kilometres after we dropped the kids at their ski hill, and we spent a day and a night on a side road, truly alone for the first time in months. Spencer and Phoebe mostly dozed in their bedroom; they felt the weight of everything but the blankets, occasionally opening their eyes to see the whiteness pressing in on me, and sharing no more than a few words at a time. They held onto one another with a kind of determination, as if they now had a clear sense of the gulf that had been opening between them, as if they stood on tip-toes, one on either side of that chasm, their bodies forming a bridge.

When the snow let up and the plough came, we headed south toward El Paso, aiming for San Miguel de Allende, in the middle of Mexico, for Candelaria Day. Months ago, a passenger had mentioned that on Candelaria Day, the first week of February, all of San Miguel filled with flowers. What Spencer and Phoebe needed was brightness.

I see in retrospect that all those months of wandering—five provinces, forty-odd states, the only stop of any duration being Florida—and every soul who had populated those months, buttressed the fortress that Fate had built against Phoebe and Spencer. Mexico was where the silences would begin to thicken, where they would first begin to resemble one of those old married couples who claim everything's been said. It might have happened sooner, and it might not have, if they hadn't come upon Norris' broken-down car, twenty kilometres into Mexico.

"There's nothing I can do," Phoebe informed him in her doctor voice, after a brief examination. "I suggest you remove her licence plates and leave her here."

"My late wife's car," Norris said. He stroked his moustache. "Yes, well then, that's that."

Norris—Norris Gabriel Azuela—had been in Los Angeles five weeks, visiting a sister. He was going home to Mexico City—he said he'd had enough of the L.A. air, he said he liked to be able to see the air he was breathing. Besides, he said, making his eyes into mischievous slits behind his glasses, he missed haunting his horrible children. We agreed to take him to Celaya, where we were turning back north. Mexico City was only a couple of hours from Celaya by bus.

Norris was settling in for the ride when Phoebe noticed the bulge inside his blazer and, assuming it was a weapon, asked if he'd please store it below with the luggage. As it turned out, the bulge was only a fat roll of currency, and that afternoon, when we found some shade to rest in, Norris proposed a game of cards, and divided his stash in three.

Just fun, Spencer and Phoebe thought, and felt like big shots at a high-stakes table. Then, when Phoebe had won everything—three piles about three thousand American dollars high, and a sea of pesos—Norris told her to keep it.

Of course she refused.

Norris laughed. "But I'm going home," he said. "I'll just print more."

Fine Arts Professor Emeritus from the University of Mexico City, Norris was a print-making specialist. Twenty-seven years earlier, in the wake of a scandal involving a daughter of the Dean, he'd been forced to resign. Responsible for a wife and three children—"graceless" he called his children—he'd etched his first currency plate the following week, carefully selected inks and papers and, in the privacy of a small studio he kept in the country, ran off his first batch of U.S. twenties. He'd gotten through the years since the calamity in the university by printing a comfortable income, even through hyperinflationary periods, even when his thoughtless children puffed up their expectations. People thought he made his living by selling his lithographs, when in fact he usually gave his real art away.

Phoebe examined some fifties, tens, hundreds, a few twenties—he said his U.S. twenties were his best. She shook her head. "No, your story's phoney, not your currency."

Norris laughed. "The curse of a competent counterfeiter," he said. "Never a soul aware the crime has been committed. You don't have to be very brave. There are no cloaks or daggers…"

∾

For a day and a half, we drove south into Mexico with Norris, a man who took more complete pleasure in every act of living than anyone Phoebe or Spencer had ever known. He relished every bite of food—the intricate flavours of the Zuñi stew, or a simple of slice of bread with black tea—loved to watch the clouds out my window, and sat for hours in one of the easy chairs, feet up on the ottoman, and made sketches inspired by stories he read in a story anthology titled *The Gates of Paradise*.

If Bernadette, Josie and Thomas were three links in a chain that pulled open a gorge between Spencer and Phoebe, then Norris was probably the one who helped them see how wide the space had grown, and the peril they were in. It was in Norris' company, for example, that they realized how little they recalled of the many places they'd visited in me. They'd taken some photographs, could list many of the towns and cities where they'd picked passengers up, or delivered them, but found themselves distinctly lacking in vivid memories. Norris called their memories Swiss cheese, called the situation a shame.

"Once time is spent it's gone forever," he sighed, and set his story anthology on the little table. "Memory is the only residue, so mindfulness is essential. Never swallow it in, just to shit it out again."

He cited recent brain research, which suggested that moments during which an erotic act were being committed turned automatically more vibrant in the memory. Case in point, his recollection of the university print-making studio the last day he was alone with the beautiful young student whose questions belied feelings beyond student-teacher regard, and which he had taken as a reply to his own queries. He closed his eyes. Even now, he said, the scene presented itself to him as if he were living it: the scent of inks drying in the winter air, the footsteps of people approaching the studio, testing the door handle, walking away; Frieda's expression as he requested she dip the soles of her lovely feet into a tray of India ink and step lightly across the bolt of white cotton he had unrolled. Feet, Norris confided, were his only serious weakness. How tender and passionate their first and last afternoon together.

And Norris recalled the most insignificant details—though more than fifteen years old, and by rights, lost all these years later—of his last picnic in the country with Isabela, his late wife. He crossed himself as he evoked her. He summoned tiny part-memories—colours of the landscape, Isabela's characteristic choice of verbs and adverbs, the taste of the wine, the texture of her blouse, her scent. He descended into his thoughts, and finally went completely into them.

It was a full minute before he returned, and when he did, it was as though he'd been dreaming, the way it took him a split-second to recognize Spencer and Phoebe. "Splendid," he whispered, his eyes moist. "A lovely gift the way these things return again and again…" He brushed down his moustache with his palm.

He claimed that his love affairs, with Isabela, and with Frieda, the Dean's daughter, were by far the highest achievements of his life. Of course his love with Isabela was greatest, though it could only have ripened as it did because of his betrayal with Frieda. The discovery of the affair, about an hour after she walked through India ink for him, was just the medicine for the inertia he and Isabela were suffering from. "It takes me off of the strictest point about memory," he said, "but it seems to me that, early on at least, no honest person can settle irrevocably on one lover, since doing so means settling on one single version of oneself. And then, we all change. We all have fears and ambivalences, and our fears and ambivalences change. Our entire way of changing changes.

"And a great love must suffer betrayal. Betrayal is the Open Sesame to a narrow doorway through an unscalable wall of ego, and inside it sits an absolute freedom. The hypothermia of awaiting forgiveness, the other's long pause of deciding whether or not to bestow it. This is the chamber where real love is created.

So the thoughts of Spencer and Phoebe returned to the night they met, and how they'd betrayed their lovers to be together. They considered their trust of one another: Phoebe pondered Spencer's present frustrations, and Spencer recalled times he thought he'd lost Phoebe—for instance, the morning he woke to find Bernadette's lipstick on Phoebe's tea mug.

"For a time," Norris said, "I was certain Isabela and I were finished. The most direct passage into our love was betrayal. But yes, memories," Norris said. "One must commit an erotic act in each place he visits. It's foolproof."

So Phoebe looked at Spencer. "We'll kiss," she said.

"Kissing," Norris nodded. "Thoughtful, joyful kissing is perfect." He returned to his reading.

So this is how it happened during those days. Ostensibly to help preserve their memories, though perhaps also for other, unstated reasons, they performed these kisses. They were mindful with their kisses, present with them to the smallest detail.

At Rio Grande, in Zacatecas, at Lagos de Moreno, they prepared for their kisses with tooth polishing and by pressing their clothes, and then, with gourmands' appreciation, explored the insides of one another's mouths. They met in the square at Silao, at noon, amid the birds: Spencer bowed to Phoebe respectfully, and Phoebe curtsied, before they approached one another and embraced.

They descended the Mexican countryside with the counterfeiter, Norris, who read contentedly from his anthology of erotic literature, and worked in his sketch pad. "What a beautiful hill!" Spencer would say, or Phoebe might note that she'd never seen a cloud quite like the one above them now, and Spencer would downshift, and look for a convenient place to pull me off the road. They looked forward to new opportunities for kissing. A different kiss to commit, and sometimes without stopping at all, merry or more dramatic, as the geography or the weather or the time of day dictated. The memories they cultured during their time with Norris are the widest and deepest of all. But it was as though the momentum that had gathered itself up while dear Norris was with us lessened the moment we left him at the bus depot in Celaya to get his connection to Mexico City, and we could see that the power had emanated less from within Phoebe and Spencer than from Norris himself. The last, snapping threads of optimism. We turned north toward San Miguel de Allende, and by the time Celaya was only a speck in my mirrors, the swells of school yard enthusiasm were giving way to an emptiness deeper than ever.

It was then that Phoebe discovered Norris' copy of Alberto Manguel's *The Gates of Paradise,* with the paper gifts sticking out. First, in the pages of a story by Isabelle Allende, a written invitation to visit him at his house in Mexico City. He said it would be good for his horrible children to meet young people glad to be alive. Second, at the page on which Manguel introduced Doris Dörrie's story, "What Do You Do When I'm Gone?," a charcoal rendering of two nude figures, one male, one female, in an embrace by a grove of trees, and signed, "Phoebe and Spencer, to perfect memories." And last, between pages 604 and 605, in the story "The Day I Sat with Jesus on the Sun Deck and a Wind Came Up and Blew My Kimono Open and He Saw my Breasts," by Gloria Sawai, all of the counterfeit bills Phoebe had won at poker, and a speck of charcoal at the line, "Then Jesus finally answered. Everything seemed to take him a long time, even answering simple questions."

The questions Phoebe and Spencer asked themselves then, as we continued on to San Miguel, and as their misery rose up massively, mysteriously around them, as they hung Norris' sketch in their bedroom compartment and knew that seeing it would always make them want to weep, were the following: First, should they go to Mexico City, and if so, what for? And second, what were the simple questions that were taking so long to answer?

∾

Splendid Candelaria. The trucks rolling silently into the main square of San Miguel all night with their well-covered cargoes, and near dawn, the drivers beginning to remove the layers of old newspaper from the plants, so that at first light the square was a sea of azalea, bougainvillaea, gardenia, jasmine, roses. Earlier, Spencer had made tea biscuits—he and Phoebe had eaten before the tower bells rang at six. So, I began the day filled with the scent of baking, and as the sun came up and the air warmed, the baking scent gave way to the fat fragrance of flowers from the square.

At dawn, tourists began snapping photographs of flower sellers and buyers, of the procession from the church. Spencer and Phoebe walked, mesmerized, through the colours and movement of the square, until it occurred to them the scene was worth remembering, and they turned to kiss, as Norris had taught them to do.

They turned to face one another, but felt a stinging sensation, as though their hearts had been pricked by a thorn from the cane of a rose plant as they admired a perfect blossom. (Later, Spencer would describe it to William as the sharp feeling of absence. Phoebe would say nothing about it at all.) They stood still there, in the square at San Miguel, and the current of the crowd divided around them, the way water separates around swimmers, until they drew back from one another with a sort of gasp. They did not embrace, but only turned and let themselves ride on the current. They would resurface in a half-hour with a bird of paradise from one of the stalls, and looks on their faces that suggested the plant was a defeat.

Then, a deep silence between them, which did not give way until after lunch, as they sat with their coffee. Spencer had passed the evening before reading stories from the book Norris had left. He picked up the book again now.

"Back to your sex stories," Phoebe said.

Her words came to him distinctly, but as no surprise. "Excuse me?" he said.

"Back to your stories. Like a husband reading *Penthouse Forum*. I imagine these days you'd have sex with just about anything that moved."

And Spencer, "What in Heaven's name are you talking about?"

"It may surprise you," she said, "but a woman can go through whole minutes without thinking about sex."

He turned back to the book.

"Any scenarios in there you want to try out?"

Keep going, he was thinking, but he said, "Phoebe, what is this?"

"As if I'm some freak of nature because I'm not your love-slave."

"Let's not do this," he said, but he thought, *Let's get this over with, please.*

She said, "Shall we have a baby?"

This had been said before, but not so seriously. He wanted the next words he spoke to sting.

He said, "A baby... And this would involve actual friction of body parts? Or would it be a turkey-baster affair?"

Bull's-eye.

A perfectly Pyrrhic hit.

I felt a swell of panic as Phoebe stormed out into the San Miguel street, and Spencer slammed his book onto the table. All I wanted was for the bleeding to stop. What was this horrible thing that lay between them? I asked myself again and again, in a dozen ways. What was this hideous, malevolent thing that moved between them, and disallowed movement, caused such systemic failure of nerve, such imperilment of their hearts? I wondered if the past could be overcome. Could the present circumstances? Was there anything, I wondered, to the idea that love in the present age is somehow more difficult than in previous ones?

At dusk, Candlemas celebrations had begun in the streets. Spencer and Phoebe had silently consumed tamales and beer in a cantina on the square, then taken a walk. Phoebe held her gaze straight ahead of herself. Spencer, feeling suddenly feverish in his poncho, jeans and hiking boots, had trouble lifting his feet, and was relieved when finally he could lean up against me, and leave Phoebe to deal with the group of local children waiting for them. Spencer's shoulders, pressed, exhausted, against me, his head against one of the yellow flowers Phoebe had painted on my sides all those months ago in Red Deer.

And I thought about the angles from which to approach love, the infinite variety of them, and how the struggle simply lasts forever. A hard-won step seems to move us forward, but turns out in the end to have taken us back. The war continues until the God of Love sues for peace, I thought. And he is a reluctant peace-maker.

Spencer said, "Let's go to Mexico City to see Norris."

Phoebe didn't look up from the children, asking to wash my windows, scrub my floors. Her words, a monotone directed toward the children, signified that she recognized the predicament we were in as clearly as Spencer did. She said, "Yes, we might as well."

"No point staying here," Spencer said as he pulled himself straight, climbed up into me, and started my engine.

∾

They drove the three hours to Mexico City and, in time, managed to find Norris' house, which was as he had described it, with its bright, white walls and lush grounds, and the servant who met them when they pulled me up to the gate. But within minutes, they learned from Norris' oldest son that his father had driven out to his studio that same morning, and hanged himself. The police had been and gone. So, for Spencer and Phoebe, the last hopes seemed to be failing. Now they knew as well as I did that the seeds of loss are planted in the most radiant beginning.

The son, Luis, was as awful a man as his father had described. Frosty, wintry, with a villainous black moustache. He sat in front of his family home, gazed out into the smoggy sky over Mexico City, popped a tiny mint into his mouth, sucked the air in through his teeth, and actually characterized his father's death as an inconvenience. The funeral, the settling of affairs, and worst of all, dealing with the old man's studio—the printing press, the plates. It occurred to Luis that he might have one of Norris' university cronies take care of that.

"My father was always a selfish man," Luis said. "He never dealt with the death of our mother, and then when his mind seemed to go…" When he snapped his fingers, Phoebe fantasized reaching over and taking hold of them, breaking the bones of them, one by one. Luis left to find his sister and brother-in-law. Norris had described his daughter as a little mouse who raids the pantry at night when everyone is sleeping.

Phoebe and Spencer stood beside me silently. Norris' death settled over them like an omen.

"Phoebe, I'm tired," Spencer said.

She said, "We can probably stay here tonight. That man, Luis…"

"No, I mean tired. Like I've gotten old."

She looked away. "I see."

He leaned back and closed his eyes. The same posture as earlier in San Miguel. "We're wasting the best years of our lives."

"No one's got a rope tied around your neck," she said, and wished she hadn't mentioned ropes and necks after what Norris had done.

I knew then that I did not love Spencer and Phoebe the way I'd loved my scholar, but as a mother loves her children. I had worried for them, tried to point them in good directions, though they'd always held the wheel. I'd have gone willingly to scrap if it could have brought them together. The air was warm, the grounds of Norris house smelled sweet. And I thought, What they'll give for a night like this when they're old and ugly and unable to walk. Or trapped by their deaths, as Norris is. They are simply unable to enjoy this! A crime is being committed. If it had been in my nature, I would have wept.

All I wanted then was for them to feel that moment as it could be felt: as a peculiar stillness in the midst of rattling, as the calm at the eye of a hurricane. Why couldn't they feel that in each step of walking, they fell through the state of balance at the top of their stride, and back into unbalance? Surely love was the recognition that the balance did come, fleetingly, and that time stopped then— an eclipse at high noon—so all the categories—good and evil, beauty and ugliness, clarity, unending murkiness— were suspended. I thought, surely that awareness was what love was.

∾

Erika. Beautiful, idle Erika is continuing on with us. When we arrived in Sedona she proposed a shopping trip to Phoenix or Tucson, or that we aim for southern New Mexico, where there's a hot spring she likes, though she's apparently willing to go anywhere. She and Phoebe sit tangled in one of the easy chairs. Erika is plucking Phoebe's eyebrows. The feeling between them has grown into a powerful, sisterly protectiveness that will turn fierce if pushed. The last hundred and fifty kilometres into Sedona, they watched an old musical on television, and when Spencer objected to the noise, Phoebe turned and gave him a sort of snarl and Erika looked at him with narrowed eyes too, like a backup force, ready with cover-fire. When Phoebe turned back to the screen, Erika did too.

A small group of people in a convoy of automobiles are waiting for Hallgren, Joy and the others at the edge of Sedona Town Limits. They will spend the day around the pool at Hallgren's mother's *Architectural Digest* house, then hike into the red, spirit-filled rocks at dusk. Yesterday, Hallgren spoke to his mother in France, and she promised to tell the staff that he was coming.

There is embracing and well-wishing, and a last-chance offer to have us join this little band, and then Hallgren, Joy and the little dog are in the rear seat of an immense, finned Chrysler, driven by a man in flowered trousers and a hat from the Middle Ages, Georgia and Boy-X are in a green convertible—no one addresses X, and one woman compliments Georgia on him as though he is a parasol and not a young man. Susanne has put on goggles, and beams from the side-car of an old Harley. Then they depart, and with them goes some of my last, lingering hope. We have no plans save to keep on moving. One destination as good as the next, the charts have all been burned. The convoy recedes at a great speed, I couldn't catch it now if I tried.

The end is coming.

∾

Our descent continues. We accelerate at the rate of gravity. The quarrelsomeness has deepened like the pain in Spencer's eye. No, he tells Phoebe, he won't see a damned specialist. How many times does he have to say it? And he dreams to himself of acquiring some special vision as his literal sight fails.

"Idiot," Phoebe says.

Erika shows uncommon courage in staying with us through this psychic terror.

Phoebe and Erika go into the Sedona bus station to drum up riders. Spencer stays here, sits at the computer, sends William an incoherent message.

The light from the monitor is like a spike through his injured eye, and brings tears to the good one. He types, and mutters nonsense about passengers we've had— Hallgren, Georgia, and ones from long ago. He is losing touch. The past feels like the present.

Suddenly panicked, lucid because of the adrenaline, he raises his face to speak to me. He says, "Bettina, the most beautiful thing I ever heard was an old woman, pointing at her little house, saying she hoped that when she died, she'd die there. Saying how happy she was in her home, that her dream was that one morning they'd find her in bed, stone cold and wheel her out the front door. She hoped she wouldn't need to leave until then."

He taps a few more characters on the keyboard, but nothing he's written makes sense when he presses

Send, and dispatches his note a thousand kilometres north to William.

"I wonder, if moving around all these months, we haven't been exploring so much as trying to escape…" he muses. "But you're my home. My roaming home, my homing…" He laughs, drifts back into his nonsense. "Where the hell are they?" he says, but doesn't look up from the screen. "The scenery is just killing me…" Madness, Love's truest nature, its inevitability.

So now, my role is to hold them as they die. Mine, the role of setting, of place: to give the proceedings beauty, and in so doing, to become beautiful.

Phoebe and Erika return with a family of mourners trying to get to a funeral in Gallup, a half-day away. A husband who washes dishes in a Mexican restaurant here, his wife and their children—a girl, eight, and twin boys, five. Taking a Greyhound was going to preclude buying meals, and Phoebe has offered to take them to Gallup for nothing. After a discussion, the man and woman counter with an offer of twenty dollars. And as Spencer pulls out of the parking lot, Phoebe sits the family down at the table, serves them stew and sandwiches—cold-clips, she calls what she fills them with. Erika sits, as though it doesn't occur to her to help Phoebe spread mayonnaise, or spoon coffee into a filter. As the family begins to eat, the radio plays a song by the Hortons. Phoebe's eyes mist—memories, clothed in melodies—and Erika goes to her.

Spencer has driven only a half-hour when the pain begins to rob of him of consciousness. He refuses to let Phoebe take over, and gives the wheel instead to the mother of the children. It's her mother who's died in Gallup, though no grief can account for her utter fearlessness at driving. Spencer sits in the seat by the door, eyes shut tight, but still feeling the light reflected off of the desert. His eyes burn, and as his head nods, he dreams of water in all its forms. Phoebe stands behind the driver's seat, as if her tense presence might avert an accident. Her eyes begin to water too, as though she shares Spencer's pain. She knows that the only chance of getting him to a hospital is to drag him. Erika, lacquering her toe-nails in an easy chair, looks up at Phoebe from time to time and smiles.

The forecast is wrong. The clear sky gives way to a dark one that pours down buckets. Spencer opens the window and tries to climb out into the deluge. Phoebe gets him back into his seat, and fastens the belt around him. One of my vent seals gives way, and soon part of the galley needs bailing. It's something the children can help with. I'm damp through and through. I feel very frail, in danger of a major breakdown.

So now, as though foretold by some Apocalyptic messenger, the Airstream merges onto the Interstate ahead of us, and I feel the same danger as before. Spencer regains consciousness long enough to notice that it's the same motor home we've been tailing for days. Phoebe agrees.

At Gallup, the family wants to stop at McDonald's, and Spencer and Phoebe oblige them. Everyone knows that people who are in mourning crave fatty food.

～

We hover on the loss of faith. Everything important and meaningful revolves around faith. Love is deserting us. We are deserting Love.

Where to pinpoint the beginning of this decline we're so near the end of? With Norris' son in Mexico City, or at Candelaria, or earlier, at some aside of Norris'? Did this present catastrophe start during our time with Thomas, or with Josie, or Bernadette, or did our naive hope begin to dissolve earlier, with some remark of William's, or on the day Phoebe and Spencer slept together, or even earlier—and here, the circle closes— with the first night in San Francisco? San Francisco is a symbol for everything—the arrival of knowledge, the crumbling of faith.

～

That ugly day we met Norris' son, Luis, we came directly north from Mexico City, foregoing the slow coastal route. We were entering the state of flight in which we exist now. We didn't slow down until the U.S. border, where for part of an afternoon and evening, I was denuded of anything not welded to my chassis by diligent border guards. Spencer and Phoebe did not have me reassembled until eight p.m., at which time they made for San Diego, stumbled onto the little outdoor café, met their next passengers.

What we pulled up on was an argument about the worthiness of a story in none other than Alberto Manguel's erotic anthology *The Gates of Paradise,* the book Norris had read and Spencer was reading now. So it was inevitable Phoebe and Spencer would join this strange group of characters, on their never-defined junket. (Once you replace the pale concepts coincidence and accident with Fate, that which clutches you tightly, it all makes perfect sense.) Phoebe and Spencer found that sitting with this group, through cup after cup of coffee, was the perfect diversion after the disturbing business in Mexico. Interesting people, engaging conversation...

Stephen was the cheeriest one. A forty-four-year-old New Yorker who had evolved a unique language for talking dirty. "So," he said, near the end of an anecdote, "while Mrs. Morrison was prying to untipper me, Mr. Morrison told her, 'Fake the yellow to the redboom.' I ted my life was saiting far me ap dome." The story had grown increasingly difficult to follow—this was part of the fun.

Stephen maintained a side-conversation about diction with George, a little, elderly man from France. George was darker in tone than Stephen; though benign-seeming at first, even grandfatherly, he was possessed of possibly the foulest mind ever enfolded. He'd been analyzed by an early Freudian and had spent the many years since excavating filth from the remotest reaches of his mind. A cultured, sophisticated debaucher. "Of course," he said very seriously at one point during the evening, in the manner of an old man in a rocking chair, "there's only one thing to do in that case: have you ever dipped your ass in milk?"

Third was Stan, the gay, middle-aged professor of classical philosophy, who would have so much to say about Eros' treachery. For some reason, I expected Stan to hit it off with Mandra, the voracious lesbian with the short, yellow hair and beret. But Mandra irritated him as much as she did everyone else, and he was far more interested in discussing Hebrew mythology with lovely Anne, a Palestinian who'd grown up in Morocco, a prostitute-turned-student-of-religion. Stan appreciated Anne's careful, earthy re-tellings of Old Testament stories, in which she made patriarchs over as human, and, to Stan's delight, turned two or three prophets gay. Not that there was anything crude about Anne—rather, she was solemn. There was something very sad about Anne, something that foretold tragedy.

Yellow-haired Mandra was not solemn. Overbearing, self-absorbed, melodramatic, she apparently alienated and repulsed everyone. She spent fifteen minutes in predatory pursuit of Phoebe, until she realized her chances were slim, then abandoned Phoebe and returned to her on-going seduction of the Taiwanese woman. It was said the Taiwanese woman had been happy enough her whole life, though obsessed—to the verge, Stan remarked, of autism—with dolls she'd made of clay and straw. Dolls with exaggerated proportions—"curvaceous," she called them, using the single English word she knew. It was, in fact, when her awareness turned briefly to Mandra's breasts that she accepted the latter's invitation to go walking. When they went off, everyone worried about the Taiwanese woman.

The last member of the group was a quiet German fellow, who was, at first glance, the quintessence of average—neither slim nor beefy, voice neither high nor low, his only distinguishing feature being an extraordinary knowledge of fashion—textiles, design, skin care. When the conversation left that subject, it was as though he stepped into the shadows, into a kind of invisibility. He actually seemed to disappear.

Conversation at our café tables circled the erotic: George's concerns about the materialist, no-nonsense approach to sex since the sixties; Anne's relief that English wasn't her first language, since it was such an appalling language for discussing sex, and would have stunted the growth of her imagination. "Dink, fuck, clit," she said softly. "So violent, so heroic. The English have a basic disadvantage. But, ah, if we all spoke dialects of Hindi…" She sighed. A remarkable, many-layered conversation.

Then, as Stephen began one of his clever anecdotes, the most striking woman anyone at the table had ever seen, emerged into the night from inside the café, sat down without a word and began to shell peanuts delicately, almost chastely. Stephen lost his train of thought and the silence was general. No one could look away from her.

"A lucky thing Mandra's not here," George murmured. Finally, when the beautiful woman popped a palmful of peanuts into her mouth, and said, in a deep, German accent that the café was going to close, everyone realized it was the quiet German man. No one had noticed him go inside earlier with his bag, no one had missed him at all. Oh yes, he said, he could switch at will—feminine one moment, masculine the next. Anne asked the obvious question—how, she wanted to know, could we know that the person before them wasn't a woman who sometimes dressed as a man, and not the other way around?

But the lights of the café began to go out, and Mandra returned, frustrated, with the Taiwanese woman, so the question went unanswered. The waiter approached with his hand out, and someone mentioned the group was heading north. At that moment, north seemed as good a direction as any to Spencer and Phoebe, and it was decided that the group would ride the Bettina Line to San Francisco.

It felt like a bad idea to me, though how could I have guessed—as Spencer loaded his passengers' things, and Phoebe invited them on board, as the spirit of the evening rose and George produced a bottle of cognac from his kit bag—that the ride would end up so devastating? That within an hour, love would be turned upside down?

I rolled back onto Interstate 5 at two a.m. To Spencer and Phoebe, the idea of returning to San Francisco for the first time felt good. Returning to where it had all started, to the place in which things had been simple. Perhaps they had in mind retracing their steps, beginning over.

They touched each other's hands as Anne told the story of the birth of Ishmael. Abraham, she said, had never been able to make love to Sarah, though his impotence disappeared when he thought of other lovers. So Sarah asked Abraham to make love to her Egyptian handmaid, Agar. Sarah chaperoned the event, guided it, in fact. It was in this way that Ishmael, founder of the Arabic peoples, was born.

In a way, Stan said at the end of the story, Abraham and Sarah's arrangement resembled a nuptial continence practised among the Swahili: a husband and wife spent their wedding night together, but intercourse only took place between the new husband and the young woman's chaperon, who thereby initiated both young people to the art of love. So Anne nodded. "Hebrew, North American, Swahili," she said. "Love is catholic."

Stan wondered if Anne was talking about Cupid or Eros. As he saw it, Cupid was just the master of technique, while Eros was mysterious. The way Eros comes and goes, enlivens a soul and then leaves it, changing lovers' visions of their beloved. Suddenly one day, the vision is all one of age and sagginess, and that's that...

George added his opinion, but neither Spencer nor Phoebe listened. They were fully occupied with their terror: the spectre of Eros shifting, his magic vanishing as mysteriously as it had begun. The lightness giving way, so the prospect of going to San Francisco—revisiting the Castro Theatre, Telegraph Hill, and the all-night bagel shop—was suddenly disgusting.

"We're very sorry," Phoebe said after she'd interrupted the various conversations. "It won't be possible to continue north. The run is concluded." When Spencer took the Santa Ana turnoff, they knew she wasn't joking. She said, "We'll pay for a comfortable hotel, but you'll have to arrange other transportation to San Franci..."

Phoebe thought she was going to be sick.

Spencer finished for her, "...to the Bay Area."

∾

Gentle Guillaume leaves us trapped. At the end of *Le Roman*, he knows that, without the rose, his life is over. "What am I?" he seems to ask, "if not my rose's lover?" But love is too fragile and confused to exist in the world. Love is as impossible as life without love. Love turns us mad, kills us.

Since the night we aborted our journey, and abandoned our passengers at Santa Ana, we have driven relentlessly to numb ourselves. We have carried farm workers to the tulip harvest on Vancouver Island, taken residents of an old folks' home to a reunion on the

Saskatchewan prairie. We've driven furiously eastward, south, north again, missing our siestas, edging into deeper ranges of exhaustion, but always moving, and always avoiding San Francisco.

Of course I am no expert in Courtly Love—I am but an *amateur*—but now I know everything. That Guillaume's *Roman* is about love as a species, that it is a statement that true love cannot exist amid the complications of the world. I know too well that the only beauty in love is the delirium of its birth and infancy. So I've cursed Love, come to view it, in its every disguise, as the most perfect evil, and further, to understand that the world is ugly too, as long as anything so ugly can exist within it. As concerns that unspeakable Master, Love, I can only say, May crows pluck out Your eyes, fire burn You, and wild dogs tear You apart.

Months ago, Norris told Spencer and Phoebe that physical love is the tip of an iceberg, and only hints at what's below. Now, it's as though a caress causes them physical pain, so they hesitate to touch.

The world is ugly.

As I've been saying, it's only a matter of time.

∾

The mother of the children was losing her power of speech as we neared her late mother's home. Her driving had become reckless, so Spencer drove the last stretch to Gallup. When we arrived, the mother hurried toward the house, and the children, infected by their mother's strain, and perhaps excited to see their cousins, vaulted out my front door too. It was left to the husband to take the bags.

∾

Evening is not far off. We've pulled off the road halfway between the uranium town, Grants, New Mexico, and Laguna. We have been following the Airstream again, and Spencer, mesmerized by its reflective magnificence, has followed it into this field, stopped us two hundred metres back of it. We can't make out the license plates, they're caught in a ray of late-afternoon sun. Phoebe and Erika are determined to stay calm. They eat barbecued chicken and swap hypotheses. "Boondockers," Phoebe says, "on a serpentine route north," and Erika answers, "A circus boss who won't travel with his freaks."

Spencer stands, announces he's going over.

Phoebe's façade cracks. "That's stupid!" she says. "You have no right to go. It could be dangerous!"

He ignores her and walks toward the door.

So she shouts, "Your eye!"

I don't want him to leave any more than Phoebe does. I jam my front door hydraulics. It doesn't even slow him down.

This is where it will end.

Phoebe and Erika drink iced tea and watch him cross the low scrub unsteadily, fine dust rising in clouds around him. They see him knock on the door, see the door opening, see him swallowed up willingly by the Airstream.

They wait. An hour passes, and then another. The day gives way to twilight, twilight to night. The only light, the moon and stars, and a flicker escaping the Airstream.

Just when Phoebe can't stand it anymore, as she stands to go after him, the Airstream door opens. She and Erika see the figure of Spencer wind his way back toward us.

"Jean and Gord Jenkins. Fargo, North Dakota," Spencer says, when they ask. "Retired hairdresser and sheet-metal worker respectively," he says. "Sixty-eight and seventy-one years old. I tried to have a conversation. You know, where they've been, where they're going, but they were watching TV, and it was plain they didn't want to be interrupted."

"So now we know," Phoebe says, but she knows it's far from over.

Spencer says, "I sat with the Jenkins in the living room of their RV, and I had the feeling that they've been treading water for forty years. That they've always made do with one another. They seemed resigned." He looks at Phoebe with his good eye, and there's terror in it.

She has to look away.

"That's us down the road," he says. "Phoebe, it's terrible."

Erika says she's going for a walk. No one asks her where she can possibly walk to from here. It's obvious what's coming. It's in the air like barometric pressure.

Erika goes, and then there's just Spencer and Phoebe.

Phoebe says she'd like to live alone. She says she might like to practice here in the States. Just a small family practice. She says Hallgren has offered to finance it. "I've always liked Sedona," she says.

Spencer says, "Sedona is nice."

"What will you do?"

"Always love you," he says. "I don't know."

"I'll head to Sedona with Erika. Find Hallgren and Joy. Maybe I'll find my cliché in Sedona…"

"Niche," Spencer says.

And Phoebe, "Yeah, my niche."

The story is over. Guillaume could not have told it better. Life steps between lovers. They will never believe as strongly in anything again.

As for me, now it's time to rest.

∾

They lie together in their bedroom compartment. Their last night together. They haven't thought of Erika for an hour, but now they hear her open the door, and step inside. They hear her slip out of her sandals, and walk lightly across the floor. She takes her robe from the closet, changes into it, ties it around herself. Splashes water on her face.

And then, I feel her look toward Spencer and Phoebe's bedroom. She stands still, facing their curtain for the longest time. Finally, takes a breath, and steps around the curtain. It's as though Spencer and Phoebe move slightly away from one another.

The air is full of a strange charge. I am aware that a single word from any one of them will end whatever is happening. Erika climbs over top of Spencer, and into the space between him and Phoebe. She lies on her side, on top of the sheet, facing Phoebe. Lifts a corner of the sheet, wipes the tears from Phoebe's eyes and cheeks. Protective, understanding. She nods at Phoebe with her eyes, and Phoebe starts to cry again. Then she turns over onto her stomach, reaches out, and strokes Spencer's cheek below his bad eye, and touches his forehead above it.

Erika sighs, and it's as though the breath from her lungs marks out a space around them.

She kisses Phoebe on both salty cheeks, then turns and, still holding Phoebe's hand, kisses Spencer in a different way. Covers his mouth with hers.

Why does she bring to mind Sarah's Agar? Or the chaperon Stan told everyone about that night? The chaperon who came to the wedding bed with the fresh, young couple? Maybe it's the way she moves: meditatively, fundamentally.

She kisses him, and moves the sheet aside. Buries her face into his neck, trades tiny bites with him, then rises slowly up on top of him, lowers herself down, and begins to move slowly there.

Her eyes meet Phoebe's and time is stopped.

❧

Dawn. Spencer and Phoebe have been sleeping their first good sleep in twenty months. When they awake, they'll find Erika gone, and they'll notice the Airstream has gone too. There will be a phantom quality to both of them.

So Eros has moved again, this time, surprisingly. And maybe love does follow its own course: maybe it rises or sinks as it performs its rites, suffers its rituals. Maybe its soul resides in the spaces between lovers, in the lacunae of a story, but now I know that explanation is a category inapplicable to Love.

❧

They have married. Soon, in the light of early morning, we'll find the road again, and in several days' easy travel, I'll see the place where my lovers began.

San Francisco. After that, they can bury me.

fin

PRINTED AND BOUND
IN BOUCHERVILLE, QUÉBEC, CANADA
BY MARC VEILLEUX IMPRIMEUR INC.
IN OCTOBER, 1998